THE RULES:

A Guide to Surviving
The Zombie Apocalypse

By Liam O'Leary

Disclaimer: Anything within this book referring to weapons and/or killing zombies is only to be done if the dead, THE PHYSICALLY DECEASED, have ACTUALLY RISEN UP and are, in fact, EATING THE FLESH OF THE LIVING. Only under THOSE SPECIFIC CIRCUMSTANCES, should you even consider doing anything within this text referring to guns or weapons at all. This text is merely intended for the entertainment of the reader...and the writer.

To order additional copies of this book, contact:
Xlibris Corporation
1-888-795-4274
www.Xlibris.com
Orders@Xlibris.com
109182

Foreword

Ghouls. The Living Dead. *Zombies.* They're *everywhere*: In our movies, our books, our video games, our comics, and now, our television series. Everywhere you look, there are zombies. They can be fast, slow, dead, and sometimes even alive, sometimes they're downright terrifying, other times, they're downright hilarious. Regardless, they're out there and they're coming for you.

It'll start with one, the first zombie. That zombie will bite someone, a passerby most likely, who will simply think the zombie is drunk or high or crazy. They'll probably go to the hospital to get it treated, but it'll be too late. While in the hospital, they'll probably bite a doctor, or a nurse, or an orderly... maybe all three. Security or the police will be called; they'll get bitten, too. By my count, that makes anywhere from five to upwards of seven zombies (Let's assume they call in two police officers or two security guards, for argument's sake) in a few hours (at most), with no one having the slightest clue why.

Now, to make a point, we're going to use some math and make a few minor assumptions: First, let's assume that it takes two hours from exposure for a person to turn into a zombie (In actuality, you can't *really* know how long it would take, it could take anywhere from a few seconds to a day or two, depending on how bad the exposure was, but for our purposes, we'll assume it takes two hours). Now, let's do the math: If everyone bitten in our little scenario has now turned (Into a zombie) and each of them bites one person, you could have as few as ten and as many as fourteen zombies, likely still with no one sure of the cause. In one day, twenty-four hours, you could have up to **28,000 zombies!** Compared to billions of living people, that number is small, but of course, those billions are spread across the entirety of the world; in our scenario, however, these zombies are all confined to *one city*. This is *one day,* assuming, **I repeat, *assuming*,** that they only bite **_one person each_!** How likely do you think it is that they'll only encounter and bite **_one person each?!_**

While I can't give you a precise number, I can tell you that it's very, very, *small*. While you're reading this, as you go about your daily routine, keep track of how many people you are around at any one time, and you'll get the idea of how *unlikely* it is that our zombies will only bite *one person*.

Let's stop and think about our little scenario for a moment: Twenty-eight *thousand* zombies in *one city*. What if what you just read...*was true?* One day, you're walking down the street and see an army of zombies marching toward you. What would you do, seriously? Where would you go? Would you try to just run away? Or would you try to find something to defend yourself with *and then* run away? If you *knew* that this was a possibility, how would you prepare? *Would you prepare?* Would you try to just hold up in your house until it all "blew over"? Would you look for a more secure place to go? Would you strike out on your own, or try to join up with other people for safety in numbers? Furthermore, how would you *survive?*

With this thought in mind, I have carefully thought out as many of the things you should do to keep yourself (at least) and those you care about from joining the undead hoard. As you read this book, you will learn what you need to do before and during a "Z-Day" incident, including what you should carry with you, what you should leave behind, where you should go, and where you should avoid, as well as what to do in the various situations you may find yourself when said "incident" occurs.

P.S.: As you go through The Rules, you may find some rules which contradict others. In most cases, these are rules for *specific scenarios and circumstances* where things *may* be even *less ideal* than they ordinarily are on Z-Day. Most of these I've taken the liberty of specifying, for any others, let common sense apply: If the situation you find yourself in tends more towards one rule than another, I'd stick with the one that applies better.

Chapter 1: General Rules

These rules are intended for <u>ALL</u> manner of scenarios you find yourself in. No matter where you are, these rules <u>WILL ALWAYS APPLY.</u>

Rule #1: Familiarize yourself with your surroundings.

No matter where you are or where you're going, you should know where you are both *forwards* **and** *backwards.* A person who knows their surroundings will know precisely what places face heavy traffic (both human AND vehicular) what places don't, and the quickest or least travelled ways to get to/from these areas. Frankly, this rule applies even in *non-*zombie situations, so, doing this for situations where there *are* zombies should come as a no-brainer.

Rule #2: Have a plan and be prepared.

While you can never know ahead of time *when* a zombie outbreak will occur, that doesn't mean you can't have *some* idea of what you're going to do when it comes. Having some kind of idea of a) Where you're going to go, and b) What you're going to do when you get there is a good start. Those who are ready increase their chances for survival, it's no guarantee, but c'mon.

Rule #3: Make sure you have guns, ammo and know how to use them.

Despite what Meatloaf might say, 2 out of 3 *IS* bad.

Rule #4: Always have a backup plan.

In a situation like this, when shit goes bad (and it almost certainly *will*) you wanna know there's a plan B...or C, to fall back on, not having one means you *may* have to fly by the seat of your pants with zombies crawling up your ass.

Good luck with that.

Rule #5: Murphy's Law.

If you are needing to use these rules, then you are OFFICIALLY in the worst case scenario, and you should assume, if not anticipate, that things have, are right now, or will...get WORSE. And if they haven't yet, don't count on them staying that way...

Rule #6: You get bitten, you get shot. Period.

This is one of the MOST IMPORTANT RULES in this book. If you get bitten, scratched, or have your skin broken in any way by the undead, the smart money is on YOU becoming a zombie in the immediate future. Neither you, nor anyone else for that matter, will do anyone any good by saying "No!", "I'm fine!", "This isn't right!", "You can't do this!" or any of the other cliché garbage often used in such scenarios. The fact is, you *WILL* become a zombie sooner rather than later, and NO ONE is worth risking everyone else becoming a zombie.

6

Rule #7: Stay calm.

As difficult as it may be to do, if you want to keep on being something *other than a zombie* you absolutely MUST stay calm. While you're always told this in non-Z-Day scenarios, it's even more important during one. When you freak out, you lose your ability to think clearly, shoot clearly, act clearly, and when you have dozens, maybe hundreds (maybe thousands) of walking dead encroaching upon you, you MUST be able to think clearly, otherwise, you run the risk of turning yourself and anyone else around you into zombies, either by going catatonic, screaming at the top of your lungs (and don't think for a minute the zombies *won't* hear you) or by losing it and shooting at your friends or letting the zombies in, none of which lead to anything good. *If* you *have to* freak out, do it *after* you've gotten FAR away from any zombies.

Rule #8: Accept your circumstances.

This goes hand-in-hand with Rules #6 & 7. If you find yourself in a Z-Day incident, the first thing you MUST do is **accept it**. Realize right now that standing around going "This isn't happening! This isn't happening! This *isn't* happening!" is only going to make matters worse (See Rule #7). All of our lives, people have told us that zombies DON'T and CAN'T exist, and this has preconditioned A LOT of people to be unable to accept and/or deal with Z-Day when it hits; this usually manifests as a disbelief that the mutilated, half-rotting corpses roaming around are really zombies, or worse, a disbelief that those *bitten* by the aforementioned people will, in fact, also become zombies (See Rule #6). If you want to survive, you HAVE TO accept that this *IS* happening, that those people running around AREN'T rioters, that they're ZOMBIES, driven only by the impulse to eat the living, and that means YOU.

Rule #9: There is NO CURE.

This is essentially an addendum to Rules #7 & 8. While some people won't let the infected die respectfully (i.e. *BEFORE* they turn) because they refuse to accept the situation, or because they're having a mini-freak out, others won't let the infected die with dignity because of some misguided belief that whatever disease that creates zombies can be cured. Let's get this over with here and now: Unless you're in a secure research hospital with the doctors/scientists who understand microbiology and have the equipment capable of *actually* curing a zombie virus, no random group of survivors is *ever* going to be able to cure it. Period. Next topic. Let's move on.

Rule #10: Bathroom etiquette.

It should be noted that while we have several advantages over zombies: We're able to think (Which opens up a whole slew of possibilities as to what to do from there), we can drive, we can hide, and we can use weapons. However, the zombies have one BIG advantage over us: They *don't* have to go to the bathroom. This, outside of being grievously injured, is probably the MOST vulnerable you can ever be, and if you're not prepared, you can easily find yourself in…well…umm… you know. Firstly, avoid eating anything that will cause you to be in the bathroom for any extended period of time. Secondly, don't go if you have even the *slightest* inkling there are zombies in the vicinity; in the position you'll be in, you can't afford to have even *one* hanging around. And thirdly, if you have to… go, bring an armed bodyguard. Having someone wielding a gun manning the door can prevent sticky situations from… going to pot.

Rule #11: If at all possible, FIND A CAR.

Cars were designed so that people could cover large distances quickly. Of course, in *this* situation, they also provide a much needed shield between you and the undead. Now, I grant you, you don't know what kind of obstacles may be blocking the road along the way, but, until those obstacles come, you are better off *IN* a car than you are *OUT* of one. It goes without saying that, if you don't have time to get *INTO* a car without getting mobbed by every zombie in the neighborhood, then wait until you find somewhere that has both usable cars *AND* a lack of zombies…making sure there's open road where you grab your car wouldn't hurt either.

Rule #12: Learn to drive stick.

Know now that the car you've used at the beginning of Z-Day may *not* be the same car you're using at the end of it. Any number of things can either happen to your car or cut you off from it, and you *need* to be able to drive any car you happen upon. When you're being chased by zombies, and you find the one working car, you can't just tell your friends "I can't drive stick."

Rule #13: Don't count on the government.

Unfortunately, the government, like most people, will be acting on the idea that what they're dealing with are *NOT* zombies, but rather rioters, lunatics, or just really pissed off people. Also, being the government, they don't have the luxury of obeying Rule #6, which means they almost *have to* take in everyone who hasn't turned, no matter how bad they might look, and will likely get what might otherwise be some of the most secure facilities, government/military buildings, turned into havens for the undead, and most, if not all, of the services they provide will quickly shut down. So, don't count on "big brother" to be too helpful for too long.

Rule #14: Don't count on technology.

Remember in Rule #13, where we discussed that the services that the government provides will almost certainly break down due to zombies? Well, the same applies to electricity, TV, radio, and cell phone signals. Eventually the people who run them will either flee their positions, die of starvation, dehydration…or zombies. While the items we use requiring these things will still be effective for a little while, it ain't gonna last.

Rule #15: Don't be squeamish.

I must once again reiterate that you *aren't* in Kansas anymore (unless, of course, you actually *are* in…Kansas), the world is now infested with *ZOMBIES*, a lot of the things you used to take for granted (see Rules #13 and 14) are GONE and your only concern is *survival*: If you have to kill furry woodland creatures for food, you do it, if you have to escape a zombie infested city through the sewers, you DO it. You'll find you're gonna have to do a whole encyclopedia of things *after* Z-Day that you wouldn't have even thought of doing *before* it.

Rule #16: NO motorcycles, unless they're your ONLY OPTION!

I don't even NEED to explain this, but I will: While motorcycles are infinitely more maneuverable than cars, they suffer one fatal defect: There's NO protection on a motorcycle, if you get mobbed by zombies while on one, you WILL die. Period.

Rule #17: Pay attention to the little things.

Quite often, people go into a Z-Day incident *with* a plan, a *backup plan,* guns, ammo, people who can use them, gas, the whole nine yards, then get turned into a zombie by commandeering a car...without checking to make sure it was "clean" (i.e. Zombie-free), DON'T LET *THIS* HAPPEN TO *YOU!!* Always make sure to check that all exits and escape routes are secured, all cars are free of zombies, all unnecessary lights are turned off (Assuming they still work), and any other little (yet still important) things are not forgotten.

Rule #18: Sometimes shady works.

There are certain kinds of otherwise "shady" behavior that can prove very helpful in a Z-Day incident. Learning, or having someone around who knows how to, pick locks, siphon gas, jimmy open and hotwire cars, can very easily save your life. If you're by yourself (Which is bad to begin with) you would do well to learn how to do these and similar "shady" skills.

Rule #19: MOVE!

No matter what, once Z-Day hits, staying put is an INCREDIBLY BAD IDEA. In the early stages of the outbreak, many people, including the government (As discussed in Rule #13), will not be adequately prepared for *or even recognize* the situation they find themselves in, and this means you're almost certainly gonna find yourself surrounded by zombies in *very* short order. Until you've gotten yourself into a far away, well secured building, staying in one place for too long is *begging* to get yourself surrounded by zombies.

Rule #20: Humanity, DON'T lose track of it.

During the chaos of Z-Day, you *WILL* have to kill zombies at some point in order to survive, and, although they *aren't human* anymore, don't let that fact allow you to convince yourself that you should *enjoy* killing zombies. Killing zombies is something you do to survive, period; it should *never* become something to do for shits and giggles. If you start *liking it,* you may be on the way towards slowly losing your grip on what separates us from them…

Rule #21: Hammers don't need bullets.

Hammers, axes, in fact, *ANY* blunt or bladed object lying around can serve as a useful weapon if firearms (Or, more likely, bullets) are unavailable, unusable, too loud (Which we'll discuss later), or in short supply. It never hurts to save a few bullets where you can.

Rule #22: Everything is a weapon.

As we learned in Rule #21, *ANY* blunt or bladed object can serve as a weapon if the need arises, but this doesn't *just* apply to baseball bats, or tools, or things like that. Anything from 2 x 4s to lead pipes, twisted pieces of steel to shards of glass, anything you can carry in your hand that can crush or puncture the skull of a zombie can *and should* be used as a weapon should the situation call for it.

Rule #23: Distance is key.

When dealing with zombies, fighting them or otherwise, you should stay as *FAR AWAY* from the devouring horde as humanly possible. When fighting them, you should try to destroy them accurately from as great a distance as you can (Being, or having a friend in your group, who is a police or military sniper or a master hunter would be *extremely* useful for this purpose) to minimize the amount of time you have to be close to them. Any such time where you *DO* have to be close to them…is a *BAD* time.

Rule #24: Keep your weapons within "The Goldilocks Zone".

As stated in Rule #23, whenever possible, keep all zombies as *FAR AWAY* as you possibly can. If you should happen to find yourself in close quarters with the undead, always try to keep them at arm's length, any closer, and you run a serious risk of being bitten. Acknowledging this, you *should* try to refrain from using short weapons that require your hands to be in close proximity with the offending ghoul's mouth. Also, some weapons may be *too long* to be practical; leaving you exposed or slowed down during fighting. For example, why use a long (possibly cumbersome) axe when a hatchet might otherwise do the job?

Rule #25: Be mindful of your surroundings.

Though this applies to all situations during a zombie outbreak, it applies *especially* when fighting them. When fighting zombies, it's very easy to get surrounded by them, don't forget there's *MORE* than one direction they can come at you from. Always be aware of what zombies in other directions relative to you are doing. The last thing you need is to down *one* zombie, only to get blindsided by another.

Rule #26: Don't be fancy!

Much like with Rule #25, this applies mostly while fighting the undead. Avoid fancy maneuvers whenever possible, there's no need to raise your sledgehammer all the way over your head to crush a zombie when a normal swing will do. Similarly, this is no time to play ninja with your blades: Just chop off the worthless bastard's head and get it over with! Wannabe ninjas...make for good zombies.

Rule #27: Keep your eyes open!

At first glance, you may think I'm just reiterating Rule #25, but there is an important difference: Rule #25 applies primarily to fighting the undead; *this* rule applies to ALL circumstances you find yourself in during a Z-Day incident; potential escape routes, safe houses, tools, weapons, threats, and hazards will be all around you once Z-Day commences. The observant survivor will see these things before opportunities are missed, escape routes are blocked and potential threats become full-blown disasters. The unobservant find themselves boxed-in, unarmed, and surprised by a roving gang of zombies. Which one do *you* think survives?

Rule #28: Know your enemy.

In the initial stages of the outbreak, there will be confusion, *lots* of confusion. You'll probably find yourself asking the following questions: "What is causing this?" "How does it spread?" "How *fast* does it spread?" "What are its symptoms?" "How long does it take to turn others into zombies?" "What abilities do they have?" "How smart are they?" "What do zombies *eat* (Other than people)?" "What else carries the disease?" "How do you kill them?" If you want to survive, it's up to *you* to find the answers to these and other such questions, otherwise you'll be completely unprepared for what the zombies may have in store for you, including the possibility that people may not be the *only* things that carry the disease. Also, by knowing how long the disease takes to take effect, you can prevent yourself from mistaking otherwise healthy (But injured) people for zombies-in-training.

Rule #29: Cleanliness counts.

By and large, zombie virus is spread through the blood and saliva of a zombie. While we already know what happens when you get bitten (See Rule #6), people often overlook that their blood *also* carries the disease, and hacking down zombies means there's a good chance you're gonna get their blood all over you, whenever you do, clean yourself off as thoroughly as possible as soon as possible. The last thing you want to do is be stupid and rub your eyes with hands soaked in zombie blood.

Rule #30: Limit your hospitality.

This goes hand-in-hand with Rules #28 & 29. Should you come across a hitchhiker, fellow survivor, what have you, be careful as to the hospitality you extend to them, and, should they show any signs of being bitten (Or maybe less than trustworthy), no matter how cruel it may seem, don't let them in, don't offer them any help, just…leave them alone. Once again, no one is worth risking your life *or* the survival of the group.

Rule #31: Maintenance.

In the event you have any tools/weapons/vehicles, you'll find that your survival will largely depend on these things working properly, but, that doesn't just happen by itself. Whenever you have a free minute, you should be doing everything possible to make sure that all of your equipment is in proper working order, so that it does *what* you need *when* you need it. Take the time to check the batteries of your flashlight, clean your gun, and make sure every part of your vehicle is in proper working order. This is *especially important* if you aren't and/or don't have a mechanic, professional soldier, or similar expert in any group you may potentially be in. If you think changing tires in a "rough" neighborhood is bad, imagine doing it when there are a hundred zombies marching (Or worse, ***sprinting***) toward you…

Rule #32: Be a good driver.

Since you'll want to get as far from the zombies as possible and you'll likely be doing so in a car, it helps to *NOT* drive like a complete idiot. Don't drive too fast, because you don't know *what* you're gonna run into (Including *other* cars), don't do anything fancy (weaving, fishtailing, fast, sharp turns, etc.) unless you ABSOLUTELY have to, and…remember to buckle up.

Rule #33: No handles.

Whenever possible, you should avoid wearing things that zombies can easily grab onto, especially things behind you, like hoods, drawstrings, etc. If you happen to be wearing clothing *with* such handles, cut or tear them off immediately. It goes without saying that wearing pants around your ankles is tantamount to suicide…and it makes it easier for zombies to grab you, too.

Rule #34: Eat! Drink! And...repeat.

While this may be obvious, in the panic that will occur on Z-Day, getting food may not be high on your list of priorities. But, if you refrain from eating, you may not have the strength you need to travel (especially if you're on foot) or fight (Do I *really* need to explain dehydration?). Of course, plenty can happen to supermarkets during Z-Day, including: Loss of power (Likely turning most of the food rotten), raiding by panicking civilians or quick-thinking survivors, becoming a haven for zombies, or even becoming a fortress for other survivors. With this in mind, the best bet is to raid gas stations, convenience stores (Both of which sell food, and may go under the radar of the mob) and warehouse clubs (Where LARGE quantities of food are sold in bulk, and are usually outside of major cities, lowering the chances of being mobbed...slightly). Wherever you go, you'd be smart to bring things that don't need refrigeration (For meat, jerky may have to suffice). And remember to stock up, as you may not find another place to find food for a *LONG* time.

Rule #35: Zombies aren't the only things out there.

As we've said before, Z-Day *IS* the worst-case scenario, and however bad things may appear, they can (And almost certainly *will*) get worse, and you need to recognize the other threats you may encounter, no matter how absurd they would've appeared to you pre-Z-Day. Amongst these are fire (The *most* likely threat), flooding, downed power lines, wild animals (including *zoo animals*), infection & disease, even radioactive meltdown. It would suck to escape every zombie within a thousand miles only to be taken down by an infection you got jumping a fence a week earlier.

> Side Note: This is a good time to remind you that not *all* of the other survivors out there may be as...*benevolent* as you are. Frankly, Z-Day will bring out the worst in a lot of people and it's almost inevitable that you'll run into at least a few. **BEWARE!** These people may want to take your food, your guns...*your life*. These people will do and say *anything* to ensure they deprive you of any and all of these things, and not even think twice about it.

Rule #36: Zombie Montezuma's Revenge

I've mentioned before the importance of water, cleanliness, and the possibility that government services may break down shortly after Z-Day. Individually, these are...*important*, **together** however, they are downright *life and death!* One of the biggest killers of people *before* Z-Day is contaminated water; it will likely become the world's *number two* killer *after* Z-Day. What you may not realize is that, without an operational water treatment plant (Previously run by the government) the quality of your water will quickly plummet, as all manner of contaminates get into it, and contaminated water leads to problems like diarrhea and dysentery, both of which are death sentences when zombies are chasing you. Worse still, a zombie, or a person *consumed* by the zombies, may find your local reservoir as their final resting place, meaning any person drinking water *supplied* from there, will turn into a zombie in short order. Make all efforts to ensure that your water supply is clean and devoid of *all* disease spreading microbes, zombie related or otherwise.

Rule #37: No help is coming.

As I mentioned earlier, the government will almost certainly *not* have the luxury of turning soon-to-be zombies away (No matter how bad they may look) so, you (And anyone with you, for that matter) should get the silly idea that "*They'll* send help." out of your mind, *immediately*. That sort of thinking is dangerous, and can force someone to stay in one place *well* after the shelf life on its safety has come and gone. Basically, you're on your own on this one.

Rule #38: Never assume. ANYTHING.

This is *extremely* important: You should, under NO circumstances, assume anything; doing so can mean the difference between life and death. The person who thinks the main highway is clear...gets mobbed zombies. The person who thinks the police station is safe...gets ambushed by zombie cops. The person who thinks their water is fine... drinks contaminated water...and turns into a zombie. You get the picture. Remember once again that this is the *WORST-CASE SCENARIO*, and anything that can get worse *will*. Just because something was safe *before* Z-Day, doesn't mean it will be safe *after*.

Rule #39: Never cut yourself off, unless you have to.

This rule, while it applies to all situations, it is especially for those poor bastards trapped in a major city during Z-Day, and is essentially an addendum to Rule #38. When trying to make good your escape, you would be well advised *NOT* to block paths unless you have no other choice, as mentioned in Rule #38, you never know when a path you *thought* was safe, even a few hours ago, may now be impassible due to zombie infestation or other similar impediment. While initially, you may think that lighting that street wide inferno or electrifying the flooded street may serve as a good way of preventing the zombies from following you, you may find out later that the path you thought you were going to take is blocked, and the only way back is now impassable, or worse, your only escape from *another* horde of zombies is now a deathtrap.

Rule #40: Anticipate.

While assumption is the avenue of the idiotic, *anticipation* is quite the opposite. In fact, this whole rulebook is designed to help you do just that. While this is important for everyone (See Rule #4) it is *especially* important in the cities. Always be ready for trouble, even if Z-Day catches you by surprise; expect resistance from zombies, expect to have to climb wrecked cars and trucks to get to the next street...and be ready to scramble *back* to the street you just came from should the other one be "too crowded". A person who is able to see the obstacles coming is less likely to get *surprised* by them.

Rule #41: Silence IS golden.

This applies both in *and* out of the city. While in the process of escaping the zombie hordes, keep quiet. You don't know how sharp their hearing may be, and the slightest sound may draw their attention. Oh, and don't be that idiot who stumbles into a rubbish can, or shoots a lone zombie they could have otherwise avoided, as things like that are *BEGGING* every zombie within a five block radius to converge on *YOU*. Way to go, genius.

Rule #42: Double-knots.

Remember to double-knot your shoelaces. When you're running from zombies and you trip over your own shoelaces, feeling like an idiot will be the *least* of your problems.

Rule #43: The Jellybean Principle.

Imagine for a minute you're heading into your nearest city at rush hour, midweek. Can you accurately estimate how many people are walking in the immediate area around you? Probably not. Now imagine that ¾ of those people are zombies. This is largely a continuation of Rule #5, and is a reminder that as you do what you can to find safety and survive during Z-Day, like trying to estimate the number of jellybeans in a jar (Hence the name), there are always *MORE ZOMBIES* than you think.

Rule #44: Comfort takes a back seat.

As you'll read later in the "Preparation" section of this book (Rule #59, specifically) and as touched upon in Rules #33 & 34, come Z-day, many creature comforts you were accustomed to prior to Z-Day become luxuries you can't really afford afterwards. It doesn't matter if you like to wear your pants "low-rider" style, come Z-Day, you'd better pull them up and have them on you as tight a physically possible (Without causing yourself unnecessary pain, obviously), or else you'll find yourself the most fashionable **zombie** in town. Similarly, you may not like to run, but, if you intend on living more than a few minutes, you'd better start running, before the zombies get you.

Rule #45: Zombies serve NO PRACTICAL PURPOSE!!

During your struggle for survival, someone (Perhaps even representatives of the government) may suggest "using" the zombies for job A, B, or C. Understand now that, no matter what, zombies *can't* be trained, utilized, or otherwise relied upon to do **anything** practical, so DO NOT make any effort to try to do so. This also means that any supplementary attempts to gather them up or collect them *for* such a purpose are also something you should **NEVER** do. Yes, you *may* be able to gather up two, or three, or four, or maybe even five without becoming zombie food, but what happens when you open up the truck/room/pen and you now have fifteen zombies? Twenty? Thirty? Yeah, you can start to see how it all falls apart kinda quickly.

Rule #46: Don't trust any government and/or corporate agents claiming "We're here to help."

Let's face it, zombies don't appear by accident: It takes a lot of time, effort and resources to create a germ which causes the otherwise deceased to keep moving and hunger for living flesh. That being said, it is likely someone with lots of clout and lots of cash created the Zombie Virus (An insidious pharmaceutical company or maybe, the government itself, make for possible culprits). With this monster on the loose, these entities need to do everything they can to clean up their mess quickly, and often, the "best" way to do this is by exterminating **anyone** who may have come in contact with the infection. This means that if you are in fact trying to survive Z-Day, they *can't* let you live to tell about it. As they attempt to sterilize the disease, they will often come posing as experts (Like the CDC, for example) claiming they're here to "Help" the local authorities contain the problem. The moment you see such people, carefully and stealthily **GET OUT OF THERE!**

Rule #47: Sunroof = Death from above.

While conventional wisdom might make you think that a sunroof would serve well as a means of blasting zombies on the move from a distance, most vehicles aren't high enough off the ground (A hummer or freight truck might be an exception) to keep zombies from climbing onto your roof as they mob your vehicle. While you (Or a member of your group) may be able to blast a few away here and there, there's a good chance that sooner or later (While reloading, perhaps), you'll get overrun, and then what happens? Either you duck back into the safety of the vehicle (The entrance to which is only separated by a pane of glass which a zombie is likely capable of breaking through) or *worse*, you get bitten, and either you (as a zombie) or the zombie(s) that's bitten you, are now pouring into the **extremely** tight confines of your vehicle. That makes for a *really* **bad** road trip.

Rule #48: Recognize the living.

We've discussed this topic in passing before (Rule #28, to be specific), but here we tackle it more fully. In your struggle to survive, you WILL come across other people, both living *AND DEAD*. Being able to recognize the (Sometimes subtle) differences between the two is crucial, both to your survival and your sanity. Remember that the living will *react* to things: as you speed towards them in a vehicle, they will attempt to shield their eyes from the headlights, hold up their hands to try to get you to stop, they will... *move out of the way* and most importantly, they will *TALK*. If you come across people *not* displaying these sorts of traits, you're more likely coming across, and that includes running over, people who are no longer alive. Don't bother racking your conscience about "killing" someone who's *already* dead...

Rule #49: Always aim for the head.

In case this hasn't been touched upon yet, now would be a good time to do so: DON'T waste precious time, energy or bullets shooting zombies anywhere but the head. While zombies' abilities to withstand shots to the torso varies, no matter what, their brain is still ultimately compelling their body to move, so rather than be the idiot who shoots them in the torso and stands around like a moron wondering why it isn't stopping them, just shoot'em in the head and be done with it. It's a…no-brainer.

Rule #50: Looting is stupid.

While I hope you're not one of those greedy, self-serving people who would use Z-Day for their own personal gain, we all know they're out there, and, should you be thinking that this is a good idea, allow me to tell you otherwise. The biggest issue with looting (Aside from proving you're a greedy jackass) is that the usual things people take, electronic equipment (TVs, computers, Blu-ray players, etc.) often require both hands to carry and can be quite heavy. Imagine this for moment.... okay? It's Z-Day, you're in the midst of a looting session, and a gang of zombies finds you. Your hands are full, and you're in a relatively enclosed place with multiple zombies encroaching upon you. If you're even remotely intelligent, you'll drop the item(s) (Which, by the way, renders this whole exercise useless anyway) and *RUN!* Also, as discussed in Rule #14, the very element needed to use these items, electricity, is not going to last very long past Z-Day, so now you've risked your life to steal things YOU WON'T EVEN BE ABLE TO USE!!! Congratulations, you...are...an...**idiot.**

Rule #51: Learn to sleep when you can.

This is tough, because, over time, lack of sleep can make you psychotic, which...really doesn't help during Z-Day. However, sleeping, especially if you have no shelter and no vehicle, can prove to be very dangerous indeed, as you may be happened upon by zombies without even being aware of it. In light of this, you should do what you can to rest whenever you get a chance to, i.e., whenever you are certain you are a good distance from ANY zombies, as well as raiders and wild animals (Assuming they haven't been turned into zombies). Even taking power naps is better than going on no sleep, which will almost certainly turn into a death sentence.

Rule #52: Try to find a secure place to sleep.

This, as discussed in Rule #51, can be difficult, especially when you have no shelter or vehicle; however, to best avoid having zombies chow down on you while you're asleep, you *need* to find some sort of secure place to sleep. If you happen upon an abandoned car, sleep in it, if you find a house, make for the attic, if you're in the woods, try to climb onto a large rock or up in a tree. So long as your potential bed won't get you killed (Sleeping in a tree shouldn't be considered if rolling over means you'll fall and break something), anything that keeps zombies from getting to you will be The Hilton compared to sleeping exposed on the ground…

Rule #53: Beware of "ghost towns".

Zombies, being dead, can spend large blocks of time (Hours, days, *weeks*) standing around staring into the void. However, should they see something, hear something, *smell something*; they can quickly go on the attack and ambush anyone mistaking areas that are relatively quiet and "tranquil" for areas that are empty. Always be wary of such places, or you run the risk of being surrounded by a mob of zombies before you even know it. This is what they mean in the movies when someone says: "It's quiet...*too quiet...*"

Rule #54: Proceed with CAUTION!

During Z-Day, you may for one reason or another find some reason to rush into areas without really assessing what may be ahead of you (**Note:** This doesn't count if you're running *away* from zombies, as your first priority will be to get as far away from them as quickly as possible), this may lead you into a situation not too different from the one described in Rule #53, where you get too far ahead, and find that you've caught the eyes and ears of *every* zombie on every street or building you've rushed past. To ensure this doesn't happen to you, if you're entering any new area (building, city, neighborhood, etc.), so long as you aren't in dire need to escape the undead as you're entering, take the time to look around, and ensure there isn't a legion of corpses just around the corner, a little precaution can't prevent more than headaches.

Rule #55: Claustrophobia saves.

Wait, what? Claustrophobia, what's that? Claustrophobia is the fear of (Usually dark) enclosed places and, after Z-Day it may damn well save your life! If you're looking for places to avoid the undead, be very careful entering dark, enclosed areas where you are unable to see inside of; these places can be havens for zombies to hide in, and, much like we discussed in Rule #54, it becomes very easy for you to carelessly stroll into such places (Garages, car washes, warehouses, etc; are all good candidates) and find yourself ambushed before you even have time to react (Which is further hampered by being dark). Once again, trying to get a good read on what the inhabitants of such structures may be can mean the difference between life and death, so, if you're not in the MOST DIRE of situations, and you start getting a bad vibe about the unlit garage at the repair shop by the road, DON'T GO IN! This is why we have fear, for shit like this...

Rule #56: Pay attention to signs.

It's almost *impossible* for you to be the *ONLY* survivor of Z-Day. Likely, as you enter a new area, be it a building, a city, a cordoned off neighborhood (Which, depending on the government's response, might be *very likely*), someone else has *already* been there and left, and you should take the time to see if they left anything behind for those who were to follow…like *you*. Simple signs are a good way for people to warn others that an area is not safe for human habitation, and you would do well to heed them. If, for example, you see a sign on the door of your local police station reading: "Go back. All dead." You can take it for certain that whoever wrote that saw the carnage that was there and decided whatever was inside was not worth the risk of the number of ghouls infesting it (Worse, lost people *attempting to claim* what was inside). It should be noted that you *can* choose to ignore such warnings, but you do so at your own risk.

Chapter 2: Preparation

These rules are intended to help you prepare (duh.) properly for the inevitable day the zombies arrive.

Rule #57: Get a license to carry. (A Gun. Duh.)

This is, unquestionably, the **MOST IMPORTANT RULE** in this section. As mentioned in Chapter 1, you never know *when* Z-Day will hit. If you're unlucky, you may find yourself in a place where being armed is frowned upon. By being able to *legally* carry a gun, you need not worry about local law enforcement stripping you of your best (Perhaps *ONLY*) protection against the undead. The last thing you need is to get busted and disarmed just before everyone around you starts turning into zombies.

Rule #58: Read up.

For those of you who lack specific useful skills (i.e. Mechanics, proper maintenance of firearms, field medicine, navigation, how to build a fire, etc.), if you happen upon a library or a bookstore on your travels (Which, depending on where you are, is highly probable) you would do well to locate books on those subjects you lack knowledge in and read up on them. You'll be kicking yourself in the ass if your gun jams up and didn't grab that gun magazine explaining how to properly clean your gun when you had the chance.

Rule #59: The best of the best of the best.

If you're attempting to comply with Rule #2 (You know, that whole "Having a plan thing"), this should help: If you have friends who possess certain useful skills (Mechanic, trained soldier, electrician, carpenter, hunter, doctor, etc.) these should be the first people you look to when preparing for Z-Day, coordinate with them, figure out how their plans and yours coincide (*IF* they do) and try to find a central place close to all of you that either *is* or can be made to be *secure*. When you're in the company of friends or relatives who have one or more of these skills, you're off to a good start.

Rule #60: Light it up!

As we will discuss later, moving around at night is bad, zombies don't sleep, and they tend to notice little things like the sound of people moving around. However, there may come a time where you may have no other choice. In such unfortunate scenarios, as unadvisable at it would otherwise be, make sure you have a good, reliable flashlight (A Maglite is ideal, as it also serves as a useful club), plenty of batteries (Not just for this reason, a bunch of necessary stuff relies on batteries, so, have as much as you can reasonably carry), matches, a lighter, and plenty of lighter fluid, so that if you *MUST* be out at night, at least, you'll be able to see *THEM* coming.

Rule #61: Don't leave home without it!

There are certain... *relatively* household items that you would (Especially if you have a group of people with you) do well to bring along, many of which we've already gone over: Gun(s) & ammo (Rule #3), some blunt instrument (Rule #21), a handful of knives for extremely bad, close quarters situations (Again, Rule #21), a flashlight and batteries or a lighter (Preferably a Maglite, which can also double as your blunt instrument, Rule #60), and a small fire extinguisher (Which we'll discuss next). But, on top of those, you'll likely need the following: A compass and map (As things like GPS will almost certainly stop working, Rule #14), a lightweight generator, some industrial purpose walkie-talkies (Rule #14), a wire hanger (Rule #18), a small propane tank (It can serve as a useful little explosive if things get hairy) and a medium sized backpack to carry it all in. If you can reasonably carry these items and still move pretty fast, pat yourself on the back, you might just survive.

Rule #62: BE PREPARED FOR FIRE!

A Z-Day incident, as we discussed in Rule #5, is the worst case scenario, so you *must* be prepared for things to go from bad, *to WORSE*, especially if you're amongst the unfortunate souls trapped in a city. With all manner of flammable materials being part of everyday life, it's very likely things may catch fire with no one to look out for them, or in the ensuing chaos during Z-Day. There may be areas that you need to get to that may be blocked by fire, or worse, you may run into what might otherwise be a dead end because of fire. In preparation for such scenarios (If it's feasible, of course) bring a fire extinguisher or fire blanket, SOMETHING that will either *get rid* of the fire, or at least let you pass through it.

Rule #63: Gas: Always have plenty around or be sure you have easy access to more.

Let's face it, the only way you're gonna put good distance between you and the devouring horde is with some kind of vehicle (As discussed in Rule #11), and all worthwhile vehicles run on gas. The last thing you want is to be out of gas in the middle of nowhere, miles from anywhere remotely safe and completely exposed (Or worse, whilst surrounded by zombies), so always ensure you have as much gas as you can reasonably carry, or make sure you aren't far from a safe source of gas, and have someone you know can get it for you.

Rule #64: The more trunk space, the better.

If you *are* thoroughly prepared (And equally supplied), it doesn't hurt to be driving in something with lots of trunk space to carry all of your equipment *IN*, as lugging it around (Depending on whether you're by yourself or not and how much you're carrying) can slow you down, or worse, serve as a handy way for zombies grab you.

Rule #65: Plows aren't just for snow.

It is unfortunately *very* likely that in your travels, your vehicle *may* get mobbed by zombies…just maybe. If you have a snowplow attached to the front of your vehicle (Preferably a truck) this can help disperse them from your path easier than just your grill alone, it also spreads some of the impact ramming them will have on your vehicle. Also, if Z-Day happens to fall during winter, and there *IS* snow…it'll help with that, too.

Rule #66: Your money's no good here!

With governments, and their paper money, likely being null and void, you need to prepare for the possibility that you'll come across *other* survivors who have something you want. Unless you want to steal it (Which, while plausible, may *not* be worth the trouble), you'll have to make sure you have ways of trading with other people. With Z-Day making certain "pre-Z-Day" items otherwise scarce, all sorts of practical items may now have monetary value, things like cigarettes, matches, beef (Likely amongst the more difficult food items to get), water (While **extremely** valuable, it may be priceless to you, trade it at your own risk), and batteries. It also wouldn't hurt to have some precious materials (Gold, silver, diamonds, even copper) to trade as well; Most, like gold, have been valuable for thousands of years, it's likely they'll retain their value *after* Z-Day. That jar of pennies in your room may *finally* pay off.

Rule #67: Could you pass the salt? (Or) I want that on ice!

While we're on the subject of valuable commodities (Including food), there are some amenities which you may *not* be willing to give up, like fresh meat (This pickiness *does* have a practical purpose, a more well balanced diet with good, fresh meat might give you a leg up on less well-fed survivors). This, of course, only counts should you happen to have a supply of fresh meat with you (Or know where you can get some). Should this be the case, make sure you have a good supply of salt or ice (And a cooler, should you have the means to carry one, obviously) to preserve it with. Without them, you may have to rely on store bought jerky and other, less fresh, forms of protein. While they'll get the job done, if you can afford to have fresh meat (Or at least, *fresher* meat), you might as well do it.

Rule #68: Plan for one.

This rule (And the following one) is intended to get your mindset on planning for *your* survival, as, let's face it; it is the *most* important thing in this situation. While I'm not suggesting you screw over a large group of friendly, sane, well-organized survivors just to save your own ass (In fact, we'll have a rule or two devoted to the *exact opposite* some time later), a smart survivor always thinks about what needs to be done to keep *themselves* alive first. Remember, as of the moment Z-Day began, you, and you alone, are now responsible for doing just that.

Rule #69: Flexibility.

As mentioned in the last rule, when planning, you should always devise a plan centered on yourself, what *you* intend to do, where *you* intend to go, and how *you* intend to survive. That being said, should you come across *other* survivors, (And if you're following Rule #59, they're likely friends of yours) and you trust them, don't be so rigid in your plan as to turn away good help, as having extra sets of eyes, hands, and guns is never a bad thing.

Rule #70: Armies of one.

As mentioned in Rule #68, you should always plan for yourself and how *you* intend to survive, and, as mentioned in Rule #59 ("The best of the best…"), it doesn't hurt to coordinate with friends who possess useful skills. With these in mind, while you *may* rely on your skilled friends, you should never count on them always being there (Remember Rule #5, "Murphy's Law"), and to best comply with Rule #68, you should do everything you can to learn what is necessary of your friends' skills from them, and vice versa. That way, if the unthinkable happens, and you lose a member of your group, each of you knows at least enough of their skills to be able to do *what* you need *when* you need it.

Rule #71: Survival is both a marathon, and a sprint. Train as such.

One of the best ways to prepare yourself for Z-Day is to treat it like you're getting ready for a marathon, because in many ways, *you are*. Even if you are able to follow previous rules about transportation (Rule #11, for example), at some point, you may come across areas that are impassable by car and, should the zombies still be pursuing you, you will *NEED* to run. Remember, zombies feel no pain and feel no fatigue, so, they can walk (Or worse, run) *forever*. Only by being able to stay ahead of them for long distances will you hope to get away long enough to lose them, and the only way to do *that* is to train your body for endurance. Train your body to be able to run for long distances in tough conditions, that way whatever your running needs may be come Z-Day, you know your body can answer the call.

Rule #72: Learn to make what you can't find.

There are certain things (Items, weapons, etc.) which, come Z-Day, may be difficult to find (Bullets, for example). The best way to deal with this problem is to learn how to make these things *well before* Z-Day even hits (And yes, you *can* make bullets). But of course, don't simply limit yourself to the basics: Improvise. There are a number of advanced weapons and items which can be made using household items. The sooner you can make these useful items, the easier you can equip yourself when these things begin to become scarce.

Rule #73: Stock up on the essentials.

As mentioned earlier (Rule #34: Eat, Drink, Repeat.) there are certain things which you absolutely *CAN NOT* live without, like food and water. These sorts of things (Batteries and bullets fall under this, too...) will be the first things to get scooped up when the panic sets in, so having a steady supply of these items will make survival, while not certain, a helluva lot more probable...

Rule #74: Rubber can be your friend, makes sure he's nearby...

When Z-Day hits, chaos is likely...no, *definitely*, going to ensue. You are either going to have drivers turning into zombies on the road and crashing into telephone poles, or having people crashing into said poles attempting to avoid the aforementioned zombie drivers...or both. When this happens, unless you want to get electrocuted, you may need to move wires, junction boxes, and other electrical circuitry in order to escape the undead. By having insulated rubber gloves and shoes (Likely in the form of boots) at your disposal, you can better avoid electrocution and maybe even use it as a weapon against zombies. Even if you can't find both gloves and boots, having one is better than nothing...

Rule #75: Plan for things as if they WILL go wrong.

Wait, haven't we gone over this already? Actually…no. While this may seem like Rule #4 ("Always have a backup plan") this is, in fact, something different. When preparing the items you will bring with you to help you survive, think ahead. Remember Rule #5, Murphy's Law? Well, prepare for things that *can* go wrong *to* go wrong. It won't take too much for backpacks to get pried away by grabby zombies, for safe houses to be overrun or for your car to become inaccessible, immobile, or otherwise incapable of going further or being reached. Whatever the case may be, if all your stuff is in there, guess what? IT'S GONE NOW!!! So, make sure you have spare items ready in the event this sort of thing happens, trust me, you DO NOT want to be scrambling around looking for water and batteries once the zombies start taking over.

Rule #76: Train yourself to be a good shot.

Much like getting a license to carry a gun (In fact, maybe even a little bit more so), learning how to be a good shot is one of the *most important things* you can do to be prepared for Z-Day. Now granted, it doesn't take a rocket scientist to fire a gun, but, it *does* take some skill to be able to shoot zombies in the head (Anything else is a waste of bullets, see Rule #49) as a troop of them either marches or sprints their way towards you. If you are a skilled marksman well *before* Z-Day (And you obey Rule #7: "Stay calm", of course), you'll be better off than some poor bastard who's using Z-Day as... on the job training.

Rule #77: Learn to shoot with every gun you have, and several you don't.

If you've been paying attention, you should already have *at least* one gun at your disposal (See Rule #3) and the means to use it legally (See Rule #57). If that's the only gun you have, and you're following Rule #76, then you're all set. However, if you have multiple guns (Which we'll cover next) it'd be smart to learn how to shoot with all of them, along with several guns you may *not* own. Why? Well, as mentioned in Rule #76, you're better off knowing how to shoot *before* Z-Day than after and the more weapons which you can use to defend yourself, better still. Also, as the events of Z-Day unfold, you don't know what weapons you may come across, they may be more effective (Or have more abundant ammo) than what you've already got, and it helps to be proficient with as many weapons as possible.

Rule #78: More guns, more fun.

As we discussed in Rule #77, it helps to have working knowledge of several guns, as you don't know what firearms you may stumble upon after Z-Day. Now, having said that, this rule also has a more practical purpose: Much like your items, any number of things can happen that may force your gun to fail or become lost, and so, having multiple guns means that such a loss will NOT leave you forced to use only your hand-to-hand weapons to defend yourself with, and as we saw in Rule #23, the less time you have to spend up close with the undead, the better.

Rule #79: Firearm popularity.

As weird as this may sound, when selecting guns to collect
BEFORE Z-Day, look around, see what guns are common
in your area and stock up accordingly. Once Z-Day begins,
these are likely to be the guns you may have to use to defend
yourself with. And let's face it; no one wants to have to run
around looking for bullets with armies of the undead roaming
around…

Rule #80: Plan escape routes.

Wherever you are (The city, suburbs, countryside, etc) you should *always* be thinking of ways by which you'll escape from these places, and that means how you'll get out of the places you regularly occupy (Your home, your neighborhood, your city/town/etc, your favorite hangout, your friend's house, *everywhere*). Of course, since you never know when Z-Day will hit, always keep these routes fresh in your mind so you'll always be at the ready.

Rule #81: Have <u>alternate</u> escape routes.

This is an addendum to Rule #80, and is to remind you that, when Z-Day hits, you *don't know* what obstacles may come between you and your escape, and, if you only have **one escape route** you won't have time to think about how you'll get out before you get swamped by the undead. Should one way get blocked, knowing immediately that you have an alternate escape route to fall back on prevents you from being trapped and also prevents life-threatening freak-outs. The more escape routes you have, the better.

Rule #82: Make practice runs.

While it's all well and good to have escape routes, you need to make sure they actually lead you out of where you want to escape. Rather than just *hoping* that they lead you out, go through them, memorize them, make sure that they take you away from where you want to get away from, and that they don't dump you off a cliff, or into a lake, or a place likely to be home to *more* zombies than where you start from. Basically, go through these paths until you know them forward and backward, and take the guesswork out of escaping.

Rule #83: Be prepared for roadblocks.

Now, despite your best prep, don't expect a cakewalk escape. If you remember Rule #5, it is *entirely possible* that *all* of your routes may be blocked by zombies, in which case, you *may* have to outsmart or outmaneuver the zombies or even fight them off to make good your escape. Plan ahead for such situations, think through all the possible ways your escape may be blocked and then plan how you'll get through it. Last thing you want is to be scrambling for ideas when your escape route turns into a zombie highway.

Rule #84: Make sure your loved ones are prepared, too.

One of the **BIGGEST** problems people meet on Z-Day (And at least the #2 reason for freak-outs) is that their family/significant other/etc was unprepared for the tide of undead which crashed upon them and...were turned into zombies. This is tough for *ANYONE* to deal with, but it can be mitigated. If you make sure your loved ones prepare for Z-Day as well as you do (Mentally, physically, etc) while you can't guarantee anything, you will at least give them a fighting chance for survival in the brutal, gruesome new world they find themselves in, especially if you aren't there to help defend them.

Rule #85: Learn archery.

Archery? Seriously, archery? Yes. When silence is at a premium, sometimes it helps to have a relatively silent long range weapon to fight the undead with, rather than alert half the zombies in the neighborhood. Considering the fact that the samurai of medieval Japan were able to fire arrows almost as fast as some guns (While *mounted* no less) being able to kill zombies efficiently and effectively with a bow is by no means impossible. With some good practice *before* Z-Day, a bow may provide a quiet alternative when quiet is called for, also, since there aren't many trained archers lying around, there will probably be plenty of arrows to use.

Rule #86: Learn to fish, and everything that goes with it.

There is a quote from Lao Tzu which goes something like this: "Give a man a fish, he eats for a day. But teach a man to fish, he eats for a lifetime..." After Z-Day, especially as food supplies dwindle or are guarded either by other people or zombies, fishing (And of course, gutting, scaling, cleaning and cooking the fish once you catch them) may be the only viable way to get necessary protein in your system, as the zombies may have eaten (Or worse, infected) all the other edible animals around. As zombies will likely be too slow to catch them and incapable of swimming, fish may be the only means of getting worthwhile food for a long time.

Rule #87: Just in case, learn to hunt, too.

This rule is really dependent on what you discover following Rule #28, ("Know your enemy"). If you learn that zombies are only interested in eating people...CONGRATULATIONS, YOU'RE IN LUCK!! Why?

Because that means they *won't* eat **anything else,** especially animals. Now, you have a very *large* supply of food which will only get better as the number of living people drops further and further. Of course, you need to know how to catch, kill, clean, skin, gut and cook them afterwards. However, should you *already know* how to do these things, and the aforementioned advantageous circumstance *IS*, in fact, true come Z-Day, you'll be several steps ahead of everyone else who does *not* possess these skills, and therefore, that more likely to survive.

Rule #88: Learn to use everything.

Remember Rule #72? The one about making what you can't find? Well, *this* is its brother. If you're hunting or fishing, for example, use the bones and antlers to make tools, or the fur for clothes. If you're camped in the woods, use tree branches to make arrows or spears or stakes. By learning how to make clothes from animal hides, or arrowheads from deer antlers, you can prevent yourself from wasting what may prove to be valuable resources as supplies begin to dwindle…especially that whole "Clothes from fur" thing. If your clothes get torn to shreds, could you imagine trying to flee zombies…*naked?*

Rule #89: Learn what plants are edible and what ones should be avoided.

While we're on this whole "nature" subject, we should discuss the necessity of dealing with plants. If you think about it, even if zombies are eating the cows, chickens, pigs, deer, etc, they're probably *not* eating things like bees and butterflies, *or* more importantly, the plants they help to pollinate. With this knowledge in hand, you may find that native plants may, much like animals, become your best source of steady eats when other food sources become unavailable. However, there are also many plants which are toxic or at least hallucinogenic. These plants, if eaten, or even touched, could sicken, incapacitate or even **kill you**. Do you really want to be hallucinating and stroll into a zombie, thinking he's Santa Claus? The only present he'll be giving you is the zombie virus.

Rule #90: Get a Swiss Army Knife.

Why does this get its own rule, you ask? Simple, Swiss army knives have been the everyman's multi-tool for decades, at least. This one item can be the thing which allows you to skin animals, pick locks, open cans, *and* serve as your last line of defense should a zombie breach your personal space. Making sure you have something which can save you valuable space in your survival kit *and* second as a personal defense weapon *deserves* to have its own rule. Also, never go *anywhere without it*…it may be your *only defense* if Z-Day sneaks up on you.

Rule #91: Be prepared for the living.

As mentioned in Rule #35, after Z-Day, zombies *WILL NOT* be your only problem. The reality is: You **_don't know_** who else may have survived. They *may* be normal like you, but, there's a good chance they *won't* be. Often, disasters like Z-Day are ideal for the more self-serving and predatory members of society, who no longer have to answer to anyone, to unleash their more vicious nature with total impunity. As such, you need to be prepared for dealing with such unsavory characters; if you're alone, have a plan for avoiding other people until you're convinced they're trustworthy; if you're *not* alone, coordinate with your group what course of action you'll take when dealing with thieves, gangs, or the just plain deranged, you never know, you may have to kill *the living* to make sure *you* remain as such.

Rule #92: Make sure man's best friends don't turn into his worst enemies.

Now, *this* is tricky. If you happen to own certain animals, like a dog or a horse, (Assuming, of course, they haven't fled or worse, become zombies themselves) you would do well to try to train them for Z-Day as well, as they can prove useful to your quest for survival. How? Easy: Horses may get through areas too rough or crowded for vehicles, and a good, obedient, dog can serve as a good early warning system (He'll likely smell the zombies coming long before *you* ever could). But, they could be a liability if not trained properly: Horses can be skittish and, like motorcycles, offer no protection if zombies get close to you, and a barking dog may alert the zombies *to you* when they otherwise may not have noticed you. The last thing you want is your dog becoming a zombie homing beacon!

Rule #93: Buried Treasure

Here's some forward thinking for you: If you're in an area where this is feasible, while you're making the rounds, walking through your escape routes, take a few minutes to bury a stash of supplies in a shallow grave (Or some similarly hidden place), so that, when Z-Day comes, you have a stash waiting for you on your escape route(s). Of course, it helps to memorize where your treasure is hidden, so bury it near a natural marker (In your back garden, if you're a city dweller, or near a tree, a large rock, if not) SOMETHING that will be easy for you to remember.

Rule #94: Make multiples of every key you need!!

Think about it, most of us use keys for all sorts of things: Our houses, our cars, our garages, our storage units, our safes, our jobs. On Z-Day, these keys might open your house, your gun cabinet, your car, a company car (Which might serve nicely if your regular ride is wrecked or lost), the back door to your work (Which may serve as a nice refuge from the undead), your gas pump, almost anything. Now, imagine half your neighborhood is zombified and advancing upon you, and you realize that in your panicked rush…you left your keys…*IN THE HOUSE!!* If you had a spare, you wouldn't have to waste precious time letting your zombie neighbors congregate…jackass.

> Side Note: Label the damn things, too! You'd feel like the biggest ignoroid on Earth if you went halfway across a zombie infested city to a place you *think* **might** be safe, only to realize that the key you have…***IS THE WRONG ONE!!!!!*** So….yeah, you might wanna label those.

96

Rule #95: Learn to build and operate a ham radio.

This is another rule that I'm sure is making you ask "What?" but, hear me out. With most of our more advanced communication systems likely shutdown (See Rule #14) relatively soon after Z-Day, you're gonna need some way to communicate with other people eventually. By learning how to make ham radios, you can have that means of communication without having to rely on more complicated devices which probably won't work anymore. Also, it's a nice backup if your walkie-talkie gets lost or wrecked.

Rule #96: Practice climbing...everything.

No matter what environment you're in, (The city, the suburbs, the wilderness, etc.) you're almost guaranteed to have to climb *something* to escape zombies; be it fences, walls, pipes or trees. So, before Z-Day *actually* hits, learn to climb anything and *everything* you may have to climb, especially if said things happen to be on one of your planned escape routes (Rules #80-82). Because, while climbing fences may be easy, what about trees? What about walls? These are the sort of things you need to prepare yourself for, you don't want some shortcoming you could have addressed causing you to become a zombie.

Rule #97: Learn to make fire.

Fire is one of the most important discoveries in human history. It allowed man to create light, become more active at night, scare predators, and cook meat. Since then, it has served as almost everything from grill, to forge, to phone; its versatility only grows *after* Z-Day. With electricity likely to fail, and fuel at a premium, learning how to *make* fire (Not just lighting something with a match, actually learning how to *make* a fire) is crucial. If you lack matches or batteries, you're going to need *something* to light your way and cook what food you may have, and if you don't know how to make fire unaided, your life just got *much harder.*

> Side Note: Putting steel wool on a 9-Volt battery can make for a good firestarter, so maybe having supplies of these items might not be a bad idea. Also, if you're in an area populated by cows or other grazing animals, their...let's just say it, **crap**, once dried, serves as good kindling, and can help drive away potentially zombie virus-spreading mosquitoes, so keep that in mind, too.

Rule #98: The need for seeds.

As mentioned in Rule #89, zombies aren't likely to spend much energy eating plants…*however*, there'll also likely be no farmers to grow or tend to those plants which we can eat. Ideally, at some point you'll find a time and place where you can begin trying to grow domestic plants yourself, and you'd like to have at least some means to do this with. Gather seeds for things that are local to you and a few for plants native to regions you may travel to…within reason. If you live on the East Coast, getting seeds for plants native strictly to the Southwest is slightly overboard…unless you plan on going there.

Rule #99: Train yourself to be your own pit crew.

We've discussed making sure your machinery, especially vehicles, are in tip-top condition after Z-day (Rule # 31, "Maintenance"). However, it is inevitable that your car will require some maintenance (Most likely a tire change, and thus, at least your original car should come equipped with a spare tire, and you should make sure its bolts aren't rusted tight) at some point, and, as mentioned during our discussion of Rule #31, you *DON'T* want to be wasting time doing it when a legion of zombies is upon you.

That being said, before Z-Day, train yourself to properly fix rudimentary problems with your vehicle as quickly as possible, when you have it down to a few minutes, do it faster, when you can do that, see if you can do it *faster still*. The goal is to be able to fix these things (Changing tires and filling up will likely gobble up the most time and are therefore, your first priorities) as fast as you can possibly do them. Speed is of the essence.

Rule #100: Have battery, will travel.

Much like having a spare tire, you should also keep a spare car battery in the event your present one shits the bed. Once again, much like a blown tire, having a dead battery is the *LAST THING* one wants to deal with when zombies are encroaching upon them. In compliance with this, one should also keep a pair of jumper cables, in the event you've found another car and have the time to jump it, or if some time ago, you had to use or abandon your spare. It should be noted that with some experimentation, one could comply with Rule #72 ("Learn to make what you can't find") and use their spare battery and jumper cables to create a weapon. Having a portable power source can go a long way after Z-Day.

Rule #101: Grace under fire.

Basically, train yourself to deal with REAL pressure. You are now in a constant struggle for survival; anyone can do complicated things when there's no pressure, but doing them with the knowledge that the fifty-odd people approaching you *WILL* eat you alive, makes even the simplest of things *MUCH* more difficult.

Rule #102: Take everything you think you'll need BEFORE you leave.

This one is short, but no less important. Before you leave your "safe house" (So long as you can reasonably carry them), take whatever you think you'll need with you. Why? Simple, under no circumstances, do you *want* to make return trips to places unless you *know* that it's safer than where you're leaving because any time you have be in the immediate vicinity of zombies is a **BAD TIME**.

Rule #103: B.Y.O.B. (Bring Your Own Booze)

Allow me to begin this rule by saying this: Getting drunk on or after Z-Day is one of *THE WORST IDEAS...EVER!!!!* The reason for this rule is *not* to get drunk; rather, its purpose is purely medical. After Z-Day, one of the biggest killers can be non-zombie related wounds which, left untreated, can cause serious infections and even death (**Note:** Running from zombies with infected feet or legs may be a death sentence in and of itself). Of course, after Z-Day, there may be no doctors to help you treat them, forcing *you* to do it yourself. When it comes to disinfecting wounds, the best way is with antibiotics, which you may not find. The solution: Alcohol. Now, while pharmacies *will* have it (And this doesn't mean ignoring them in your search), they may be cleaned out, overrun or destroyed before you can get to it. However, most homes will carry some form of alcohol which can serve your medical needs without necessarily having to search potentially dangerous places to get it. Also, there likely won't be *too many* zombies in your local liquor store after Z-Day...

Rule #104: Brace yourself...shit just got real.

This...this is simultaneously one of the most important rules in this section, and also, one of the most difficult to actually carry out. Z-Day guarantees you will see **the most horrific things human eyes could ever see.** Z-Day will be Hell on Earth, you will see the dead walk and consume the flesh of the living, you will almost certainly see everything you've ever known go down in flames (In some cases, literally), practically everything which had previously brought you comfort will be destroyed, you will see people (Likely even people you care about) eat their own friends, neighbors, and family, and whatever preconceived notions you had of your future will turn to dust in the wake of the utter chaos Z-Day will usher in.

As difficult as it may be, you need to find a way to get your mind prepared for this living nightmare and be able to cope with it, if you can't you'll disobey Rules #7 AND #8 ("Stay calm" and "Accept your circumstances", respectively) and essentially resign yourself to joining the undead.

Now, how do you prepare? *This* is where things get difficult. The best thing I can advise is:

1) Have faith in something. Even if people around you may think it's pointless to believe in something after Z-Day, if it helps *you* keep your head, they can **shove it**. If you find that you have to put down a cherished friend or loved one, force yourself to think of it as sending them to a better place, away from the Hell *you* find *your*self in.

2) Keep hope. Later in this book, we will discuss long term plans for life after Z-Day. You need to know, not "think", **<u>KNOW</u>** that if you can survive, you can attempt to rebuild something resembling civilization, and *maybe* find a way to turn the tide against the undead.

3) Imagine the worst thing (**THE *WORST* THING**) that could happen on Z-Day, then, remember that this almost certainly **<u>will</u>** happen. If you can cope with whatever horror you envision, you *might* be on the right track.

Chapter 3: Procedures, Procedures, Procedures

Certain rules, while they may work at certain times in certain places, may be a death sentence somewhere else. This chapter will cover the how, where, and when of such rules.

Rule #105: Don't go out at night.

<u>Situation: You find yourself in the country, or some slightly wooded suburbs.</u> **Note**: This does *NOT* apply when you're in the city.

While staying mobile is key to your survival, you need to be logical: Wandering around blindly at night is stupid *without* zombies, **with** zombies, it's downright suicide; if you have even a *relatively* secure home base, *STAY THERE* until sunrise. Incidentally, don't think a flashlight will save you (Though, this *isn't* to say you *shouldn't* bring a flashlight). Just let me ask you this question: Do you know what a random light appearing out of nowhere means to a zombie?

*Dinner...*the answer was dinner.

Rule #106: Suspension of Disbelief

Situation: You are watching TV or something on the internet, and catch something that looks suspiciously like… **zombies**.

Rule #8 (Accept Your Circumstances), is intended for those in the thick of Z-Day. *This rule* is for those…*not* in the thick of it. While Z-Day *can* sneak up on you, there is an equally good chance that you may see it coming, even if you don't realize it. If you catch some videos showing a very *realistic* display of the dead walking (Or taking bullets), TAKE IT SERIOUSLY!! Denial is one the biggest killers on Z-Day: It leaves otherwise capable people totally unprepared and can make their preparations begin too late to be useful. So, the moment you see said footage, you should begin preparation mode (See Chapter 2: Preparation), because, if you're seeing footage of it, it won't be long before it's on your doorstep.

Addendum: Should you see/hear a report where the reporter actually *uses* the "Z-word", or describes something which can be reasonably believed to be a description of a zombie attack (Severely wounded people getting back up, cannibalistic behavior, extremely violent, unprovoked rioting, etc.), allow me to say this, before you even utter it in your inner monologue: This…will…*NOT*…***BLOW…OVER!!!!*** If you are seeing this, you have just been given a rare opportunity to see the zombies coming before they've arrived on your doorstep, if there was *ever* a time to flip to the "Preparation" section of this book *NOW* would be the time to do it!

Rule #107: Avoid major cities like the plague they're infested with.

Situation: You started Z-Day _anywhere_ but a major city.

In situations like this (i.e. Zombie-related situations), remember this equation:

$$\text{Places with lots of people in confined spaces}$$
$$=$$
$$\text{Places with lots of } ZOMBIES \text{ in confined spaces}$$

If you're _not_ in a city, good, you're off to a good start, the population is likely more dispersed and a little bit easier to avoid and the zombies will likely need more time to congregate into dangerous numbers. However, should you find yourself in such a place when Z-Day arrives, you need to GET OUT as quickly as possible, because, well, look at the equation! _You_ are now in a place with lots of zombies... in confined spaces. Do the math.

Rule #108: Avoid major HIGHWAYS like the plague, too.

<u>Situation: You are trying to get around on/after Z-Day and you may or may not be fortunate enough to have a working car.</u>

People drive like lunatics under *normal* circumstances, and these circumstances are *FAR* from normal. Between people turning into zombies while driving, having someone *in their car* turn into a zombie while they're driving, running into a horde of zombies infesting the highway, and just the chaos on the highway that comes with this sort of a situation, it's almost impossible NOT to run into roadblocks on the highway, and no matter what, you CAN'T afford to backtrack. Worse still, if you have a roadblock, anyone sitting in their car is literally a "sitting duck" just waiting for any zombies to rip them out of their cars and chow down. Dead end indeed.

City Rules

The next few rules are all for those poor souls who find themselves trapped in a city when Z-Day hits, and are thoroughly unprepared for it. May God have mercy on their souls...

Rule #109: Don't go towards the light.

Situation: You find yourself trapped in a zombie-infested city <u>*at night*</u>.

This is a rule which is intended for the unique circumstances survivors in the city will likely run into. It should be noted that in cities, especially on the first few nights following Z-Day, Rule #105 ("Don't go out at night") goes out the window; as your home may be a veritable deathtrap due to the fact you're in the close confines of a city. With that in mind, you might do well to use the cover of darkness (**Note**: You *can* go out during the day, but remember, in the daylight, you're as easy for them to see as they are for you). Now, *that* being said, while avoiding *total darkness* (Like in some alleys and tunnels for example) is indeed something you should adhere to, staying beneath streetlights is *equally (If not MORE) dangerous,* since the light will make *you* just as easy to see as the zombies. Think of those old movies where the crook gets caught by the spotlight...now throw in zombies.

Rule #110: Get out of sight.

Let's begin by saying: If you're in this situation…it's bad, it's real bad, it's *WICKED BAD*! You DO NOT want to find yourself in this mess, because you've probably got dozens of zombies taking a bite out of everything that moves, clogging the streets and the carnage you're seeing may be pushing you dangerously close to freaking out. Now, if you plan on surviving, you have to run, and you have to run hard, the more distance you can put between you and them, the better. Now, while you may not know how *else* they may detect you, you can know for sure that if they see you, they *WILL* come for you, ***do not** let them see you!* When you're running, turn corners, duck down alleys, whatever you do, make sure they don't see where you've gone, if they do, you can bet they'll just keep following you. In those first few minutes from the onset of Z-Day, hopefully, (As bad as this may sound) there will be other people around to keep them distracted, so that once they lose sight of you, they'll quickly move on to something else…

Rule #111: If at all possible, find a weapon.

While running away from the zombies is obviously the only way you'll escape them, it's painfully evident that, in order to survive, you will, sooner or later, have to kill some of them; therefore, you need something to do it with (You run too much risk of infection trying to do it with your bare hands). Luckily, cities contain millions of things to bash a zombie's brains in with. If you are not in immediate danger of being overrun by the undead, take a minute or two to grab something: An axe, a crowbar, a baseball bat, a hammer, a knife, whatever you can get your hands on, so long as it's hard enough to scramble some brains and just long enough to keep them from gnawing on your hands. A bit of advice: At this point in the disaster (When Z-Day officially hits and everything goes to shit), there will be so much chaos, noise won't be a problem, so, if you're anywhere where a gun is likely to be found, go and get one. Remember Rule #23, the further away you can kill zombies from, the better.

Rule #112: Find shelter...<u>FAST</u>!!!

This fits in quite snugly with Rule #110 ("Get out of sight"). If you're scrambling to avoid the undead, getting inside, quickly, is the best thing you can do...*however*, you DO NOT want to be *spotted* entering a building if you can help it, because it's highly likely that the zombies will either try to wait you out, or worse, try to follow you *in* (Which we'll discuss the dangers of *that* later). With this in mind, you may want to avoid choosing buildings with large glass facades for your shelter, as they will scream "HEY! I'm going into ***THIS BUILDING!! FOLLOW ME!!!!!***"

Rule#113: "...umm...I'll take...the stairs".

This is a slightly double-sided issue, to be honest. On one hand, you have the speed of elevators, which is important; you may find yourself in a tower with HUNDREDS of floors, and walking up and down all the stairs, which can be, especially if food and water are tough to get, *extremely tough* on your body, and drain you of energy you'll need for fighting or fleeing zombies. On the *other hand* elevators, especially at the onset of Z-Day, are an ambush *WAITING* to happen. Think about it: If one person turns whilst on the elevator at say the 25th floor, they could easily, by the time they reach the lobby, be joined by another half dozen zombies!!! If you're unarmed and unprepared, you will need lightning reflexes to avoid getting swarmed by the undead as they launch themselves at the sound of the ding; what's more, if the zombies aren't waiting for you *IN* the elevator, they may be waiting for you *AT* the elevator, which is even **worse.** Remember, elevators are tight and have narrow doorways, and any zombies on your floor immediately have something which you *may not* have: The advantage of *knowing* you're coming. By taking the stairs, you can at least get *some* idea of what might be waiting for you. On the elevator, the ding sounds more to the zombies...like the dinner bell.

Rule #114: Stay low.

Most, if not all, cities have skyscrapers; some can reach many hundreds of feet into the air. At first glance, these can seem like the perfect places to hide from the undead. But, let's think about this for a minute: First, as discussed in Rule #113, ascending them is far from easy. Second, and more importantly, if you're unfortunate enough to be residing in one alongside some zombies, or they follow you inside, you now have a huge problem on your hands: From the 3rd floor and up, if you needed to, could you survive jumping from these heights? The reality is, if zombies or fire cut you off from the first two floors, you are in *DEEP TROUBLE*; you will be unable to reach the ground again without serious risk of zombie infection, burning, grievous bodily harm, or…certain death. And, as you relinquish more floors to the advancing zombies, your chances of escape shrink rapidly. Whatever you do, try as best as possible to maintain control of the first two floors of any skyscraper, or risk entering a deathtrap.

Rule #115: The likeliest of places.

At the onset of Z-Day, certain places, due to the high volume of traffic they will likely attract, are places to avoid (Highways are a perfect example, Rule #108). However, some places, which you may *think* might be bad places to go to may, in fact, be a viable base of operations, at least for a little while... among these are police stations. As Z-Day *WILL* be chaotic, most of the police will likely either be trying to quell the situation OR they will be trying to turn the station into a fortress to hold off the undead. If you can get in without getting shot, the police may even deputize you in an attempt to hold the station. Just make sure the police know what they're dealing with first...the last thing you want is to find out that the holding cells are now a zombie zoo.

Rule #116: The unlikeliest of places.

Let's be honest: There are some places in most cities you *don't* wanna go. Why? Violence. *GUN VIOLENCE*. Areas which earn this reputation do so because criminals go around shooting each other, and often, hit innocent people in the process. While this makes them places to avoid normally, it also makes them places you should consider *going to* on Z-Day, since the criminals may be a little more prepared for Z-Day than everyone else (At least, better at shooting zombies anyway) and certainly will be better armed than your average city dweller. Considering the extreme circumstances of Z-Day, if those criminals are trying to defend themselves against the undead, they *may* be willing to take any help they can get, even from unlikely sources. Just remember to stay on your toes: Criminals may not be so willing to turn off their more predatory traits when things get bleak. Even if they're unwilling (Or unable) to help you fight zombies…at least they'll probably have plenty of guns.

Rule #117: Go where the guns are.

This is another tricky one, as other people may have the same idea, but, once you've managed to elude the initial swarm of undead on Z-Day, do what you can to get to a place you *know* has guns (See Rules #115 & 116). Gun stores, military barracks, police stations (A la Rule #115), *any* of these places should be searched so long as you're capable of doing it. While you *may* be able to get by without certain things, being unable to defend yourself *is NOT* one of them.

Rule #118: Use technology while you still can.

As mentioned way back in Rule #14 ("Don't count on technology"), the events of Z-Day may cause much of our modern technology to become useless in fairly short order. However, it's a safe bet that during the earliest hours of Z-Day, this will *not* be the case. While you still have the opportunity, use your phone, PDA, whatever you may own, and use it to pull up maps pointing you to wherever you need to get to, be it a hardware store, gun store, police station, **wherever.** While you're at it, do what you can to warn others what may be waiting for them, no point in letting people you care about get turned into zombies if it can be avoided. Any advantage you have should be used so long as it's available to you. At least you won't have to worry about being charged for data…

Rule #119: Don't follow the crowd.

This is important: The moment Z-Day hits, there *will* be mass panic, with people running for the exits (Major highways [See Rule #108], bridges, tunnels, train terminals, etc.) in droves. What you may not realize, especially if you happened to ignore Rule #7 ("Stay calm"), is that panic is one of the biggest killers on Z-Day: Panic causes people to act without thinking, like…running into an oncoming truck to avoid the zombie chasing them, *or*, (And this is where you should *really* be paying attention) it can cause people to disregard the welfare of others, which often manifests as people being **trampled to death** by the panicking mob as they reach inevitable bottlenecks (The entrance to a train heading out of the city is a likely one). This, and a worse fate, <u>not</u> being trampled to death, can be avoided by figuring out where the crowds are likely to go for sanctuary/escape and ***avoiding*** them. And yes, if a panicked crowd has gathered around the nearest police station, this rule <u>negates</u> Rule #115.

Rule #120: Avoid public transportation.

This is another no-brainer. Assuming they're still running (Considerably likely in the first few hours of Z-Day), buses and trains on Z-Day, much like elevators, can easily become coffins on wheels at breakneck speed: All they need is <u>one</u> passenger to zombify to turn a mass escape vehicle into a party bus for the undead. So, the moment you see anything leading you to believe your city has a zombie problem, avoid buses *and especially avoid* subways. Unfortunately, with the likelihood of there being major zombie-related traffic jams, vehicles may not help you terribly much and you're likely to be more maneuverable and therefore easier to escape, if you're on foot. Now if, on the very slim chance, you're being chased by a few hundred zombies down your city's main drag and a bus happens to drive by, then okay, but otherwise, the risk is too high that someone on the bus will turn and wreak utter havoc on all inside to make them a viable means of escape.

Rule #121: To the sewers, quick!

Remember back in Rule #15, when I said "Don't be squeamish"? Yeah...*this* is one of the reasons why. With most of your conventional exits likely crowded by a panicking mob which will turn into *a zombified mob* in relatively short order and probably remaining so for a while, your best bet for escape may be in the area likely to be the *least populated*: The Sewers.

Let's think about it for a minute: The sewers are, well... sewers, it doesn't need much further explanation than that, does it? How many people do you know who live in the sewers? Do you even know of any *homeless people* who reside in the sewers? With these thoughts in mind, it's a safe bet you can rely on *very few* people living in the sewers and even fewer having the wherewithal to think of escaping through them. You may have to wade through...you know, but that's a helluva lot better than turning into a zombie.

Rule #122: Grab a light.

So long as zombies are not right on top of you, if you're anywhere near a convenience or hardware store, grab a flashlight or lighter(s), as you're definitely going to need them sooner or later, especially if you plan on following the previous rule. Also, as mentioned in Rule #60 ("Light it up"), certain flashlights are heavy enough to use as a club if the situation should call for it, and any versatile weapons are weapons worth having. You may not need it all the time, but you're gonna need it eventually, and it's better to have things you *may not* need than to be lacking something you'll *definitely* need.

Rule #123: Safety in numbers.

As you make your way through the city you'll inevitably need *something* (Gun, flashlight, hatchet, etc.) otherwise you may find yourself stumbling around blind and defenseless. Now, logic may make you think that your best bet to retrieve these essentials would be to wait until the panicking crowds have dissipated, but you'd be **wrong.** If you wait, while those crowds may no longer be panicking, they're certainly not gone: They've become a whole *new* legion of zombies waiting for a lone scavenger to wander into their neighborhood. Rather than wait for the living to become zombies, go immediately. Yes, you'll have to avoid both zombies and the panicking masses, but those panicking masses will also divert the attention of the (Comparatively fewer) zombies. As cruel as it sounds, sometimes the only thing you need to survive is to be faster or more agile than the guy you just passed.

Rule #124: Avoid train tunnels.

Whether or not you're following Rule #121 ("To the sewers, quick!"), you would be wise to avoid trying to travel through train tunnels. As mentioned in Rule #120, public transit (Which definitely includes trains) can become a virtual deathtrap on Z-Day, needing only one passenger to zombify to turn the entire vehicle (Be it a bus or, in this case, a train) into a giant can of undead. This being the likely case, it's almost impossible for the possibly hundreds of zombies *not* to spill out of the train eventually, leaving the tunnels with a veritable small army of ghouls which, in the dark, is certain doom.

> Side Note: Not even having a flashlight will help, as mentioned in Rule #105 ("Don't go out at night"), in situations like this, it'll only *draw them to you.* DO NOT ENTER!!!

Rule #125: A walk in the park.

This is (Yet another) tricky rule. Parks…being…parks, are naturally open, ideal for avoiding zombies, giving you plenty of room to dodge and weave around the undead. *However,* that openness also means that any zombies in the surrounding area can notice you very easily, meaning that instead of potentially having only a handful of zombies pursuing you, you may have *hundreds.* So, use your best judgment when entering, if there aren't a lot of zombies in the outlying areas, then go; if there are tons of zombies around, you may need to (If its viable) find another way around or risk being spotted by them.

Rule #126: Do NOT feed the animals!!

Z-Day will be chaos, and part of that chaos, especially in this scenario, means that you won't have time (Or the means) to find out what else is susceptible to zombification (Rule #28, "Know your enemy"). With this in mind, any areas where there *may be*, not to mention where there *definitely are*, wild animals should be avoided as best as possible. I mention this because if you should find yourself in a city park (Rule #125) many of them, New York's Central Park, specifically, comes to mind, also house the city's zoo, which will be populated with myriad exotic animals which could potentially be zombified (And, like people, likely be released from the physical limitations they used to face while they were alive). With this being a possibility, you should avoid zoos as best as you can. Even if initial scouting reveals no zombie animals, you don't know what you'll find further in, and the last thing you want is to get within sight of the exit, only to be mauled… by a zombie gorilla.

Rule #127: Do whatever you can to escape the city as soon as possible.

This is basically Rule #107 ("Avoid major cities...") from the *other* end. While the reasoning behind this may seem obvious, (Lots of zombies, tight spaces, the whole nine yards) there is *another* factor you may not think of that makes the need to escape **MUCH MORE URGENT**: If they realize what's going on, nuclear armed governments may deem the situation so bad as to consider "The Nuclear Option", by which they'll destroy the city (And *everyone* in it) to prevent further contamination. Should this become a possibility, (Which frankly, you *must* assume) you *will* have a **very limited time** to escape and this makes staying in the city for very long *incredibly* **<u>dangerous</u>**.

Note: This does *NOT* negate Rule #119 ("Don't follow the crowd"). In fact, this *may* even reinforce Rule #121 ("Get to the sewers..."), as they **may** provide *some* (Repeat: **<u>SOME</u>**) protection against the nuke. Anything's better than being on the surface when it goes off...except, of course, zombies.

Rule #128: Don't get attached to your ride.

Way back in Rule #11 ("If at all possible, find a car"), we covered the need for a car, the obvious reasons being the natural protection they provide and their ability to outrun even the fastest zombies. However, *this* section (As it's the one setting where you're *most likely* to need to) details the need to be ready to *abandon* said vehicle the moment it's unable to elude zombies. As Z-Day breaks, cities will be utter chaos: Major exits become parking lots or demolition derbies (…Or both) and the streets will be pandemonium. It's very likely that eventually, something will slow you down, making you vulnerable to zombie ambush. If this happens, you need to ditch your vehicle **immediately**. Much like staying in one place too long, staying in a car beyond its usefulness is a REALLY BAD IDEA, one that will get you a one way pass into Club Zombie. On the plus side, you're almost guaranteed to find another usable abandoned car eventually. So, once you reach a point where your car isn't useful, bail. Make a run for it, lose the ghouls and then…find another one!

Suburban Rules

The following rules apply to those who find themselves in the suburbs when you discover Z-Day has arrived and (Again) are **not** prepared for it (Although, if you've been following along with Chapter 2, you really should be...but I digress). As suburbs have different layouts and different population density, the rules for them are **not** <u>necessarily</u> the same as those in the city, though for our purposes, assume them to still be rather tightly packed and somewhat densely populated.

Rule #129: Unless you live in a virtual fortress, DON'T STAY PUT!!!

During the earliest hours of Z-Day, things will be chaotic. But, much like in the cities, there will likely be more humans than zombies, and that means there's a good chance you'll have the time and space to escape your home before it quickly becomes mobbed by the undead. This, especially if it's only one floor, can soon become a *very menacing* threat, and the longer you wait, the more the ratio of humans to zombies flips around. If you wait too long, you may find yourself trapped with what *used to be* your neighbors attempting to eat you alive. **Note**: If you have a large home (Preferably with two floors and an attic; we'll discuss the importance of attics later) with a good solid fence, staying put *may not* be such a bad idea, so long as you have the means to live (Food, water, etc.) and defend yourself, you could find that your home *may*, in fact, be a *good place* to ride out the worst of Z-Day. No point in ditching a solid shelter if you don't have to.

Rule #130: Stick to main roads whenever possible.

As mentioned at the beginning of this section, suburbs can be surprisingly tightly packed: Houses can sometimes be separated by only a few feet of grass or shrubs, neighborhoods can have several dozen houses on them before you reach a main road and each house can be occupied by as many as seven people or more; you start doing the math and you realize, being in the suburbs on Z-Day is no picnic. With this, as well as Rules #53 & 54 ("…Ghost towns" and "Proceed with caution", respectively), in mind, you would be wise to stick to the wider main roads (Which almost certainly give you more room to maneuver), as in the relatively tight confines of the side roads, you can quickly find yourself boxed into a situation you can't get yourself out of. Imagine running into a mob of zombies or a car pileup and then trying to make a three-point turn on residential roads…yeah…those prospects *are not* good.

Rule #131: Beware of other drivers.

This is an addendum to Rule #32 ("Be a good driver"), and is given in *this* section because driving in the city when Z-Day hits is, while just as dangerous, likely to be for shorter times and over shorter distances. In the suburbs, on the other hand, you may go over large spans of distance and time in a car, and in doing so, run a greater risk of running into other vehicles in that time. So, while you ride around in the suburbs, be very alert, other survivors *may not* be as stable as you and may be freaking out behind the wheel, focusing so much on making sure the undead swarm is not behind them anymore, that they may fly through intersections at frightening speeds, obliterating anyone or anything that happens to be in their path…like you. Whenever possible, keep your eyes open for any vehicles barreling towards you from any direction. Alert drivers are a hell of a lot more likely to survive in the racetracks of the suburbs than oblivious ones.

Rule #132: "All the kids do it!"

It is a common practice by children and teenagers to cut through their neighbors' back yards and use them as shortcuts; on Z-Day, this tactic can also serve *you* as you attempt to evade the undead. Think of this for a moment: On Z-Day, the majority of the zombies will be roaming the streets and will have a very good view of *the fronts of the houses* in the neighborhood. However, their ability to see *the rears* of the houses will likely be impeded (Unless of course, you live in a neighborhood which has wide gaps between houses, in that case you may have to cut through to the back yard *perpendicular* to your house instead of the ones *parallel*, which is the method being implied here), meaning that, if you're fast enough, quiet enough and (Relatively) stealthy enough, you can sneak through the back yards of the entire neighborhood without drawing the attention of the undead!

Side Note: Certain outside factors can help or hurt you in trying to carry this out, for example: Yards surrounded by relatively high fences, be they wood, stone, concrete, brick, or shrub, can provide you with adequate cover to slip over and into the next yard without being seen. Conversely, if the zombies are surrounding the house, you may want to find a different method of escape, as they could possibly grab you trying to get over/through the fence. To avoid such scenarios, try to look over/through the fence and see what's waiting for you on the other side before you hop it.

Rule #133: Lock yourself IN your car.

Wait...what? That's right, you read that *correctly*. As you drive around your neighborhood on Z-day, make sure your doors are thoroughly locked and your windows rolled up, not because the zombies are necessarily going to open your doors and climb in (Although you shouldn't think they won't try...) but because, if they catch you off guard, *other survivors* may attempt to rip you out of your car and leave you for dead. DON'T LET *THIS* HAPPEN *TO **YOU!!!*** By locking yourself in your car, their attempts to rip open the door (Likely the first thing they will try to do) will fail...miserably. Now, if you haven't noticed by now someone trying to pry open your door...this text can't help you because you have the observational powers of a rock. Otherwise, seeing someone attempt (And fail) to open your door will give you time to speed away before they go back and get a rock to smash your window in with. Just remember to unlock your doors when you want (Or more likely, *NEED*) to get out.

Rule #134: Avoid town centers whenever possible.

Most centers of most towns are where there is likely the highest population density at any one time (I know, I know, *malls*, but we'll get to that later) due to most traffic having to pass through to get to and through most points of interest in town. On Z-Day, this may prove to be a huge problem, as your town center may be jammed with crashed or abandoned cars from the panic of the zombies' arrival, *or worse*, filled to the brim with zombies. Not surprisingly, this can easily become a deathtrap and therefore, should be avoided as best as possible; while this may not be entirely feasible, as most towns' main drags cut through the center, most also intersect other main roads along the way. Should this be the case, TAKE THOSE ROADS!! It's almost impossible to NOT be able to circumnavigate the town center by following the other main roads in town eventually. Yeah, this might burn gas and take a little while longer, but if it means avoiding a wave of zombies...trust me, you'll thank yourself later.

Suburban Rules, Sub-Section: Mall Rules

Yes, that's correct, <u>Mall Rules</u>. Malls are relatively small environments unto themselves but are also likely to be fairly densely populated, and as such, have their own set of rules which need to be carefully observed. Much like with the others, assume for our purposes that you find yourself in your local mall (Which we'll assume is in a suburb of your nearest major city, though even in the city, the rules are roughly the same) when Z-Day falls and, again, you find yourself <u>completely</u> unprepared for it.

Don't look so surprised...you knew these were coming eventually.

Rule #135: Make for the exit!!

This is an ABSOLUTE NO-BRAINER. If you stroll into your local mall and catch even *THE SLIGHTEST HINT* of zombie activity... RUN! Make for your car (Preferably in the parking lot closest to your entrance) and get out of there **_AS QUICKLY AS POSSIBLE!!_** The longer you take to do this, the less likely you are to get out alive, as with each second, more people are becoming zombies and those who aren't are likely in panic mode, potentially causing traffic jams and pileups at the exits. So, to reiterate: Get out, *FAST!!!!*

> Side Note: Parking in the garage may complicate this... *considerably.* In the garage, because of its tight spaces, volume of cars, distance from the ground and the fact it is enclosed, your means of escape is far more constricted and therefore, more difficult to navigate than a regular parking lot (Which itself is no picnic). If you're parked here, you may need to move even faster if that's possible, as any panicking motorist here are likely to spell certain doom for everyone else, because they will likely choke exits with wreckage. With this in mind, you would be well served to a) Park in a parking spot as close to an exit as possible and b) *BACK INTO* said parking spot, if you can avoid unnecessarily wasting precious time backing out and having to correct yourself, the better. This *would* be a rule, but we're assuming you're completely unprepared in this instance *and* this is too specific to place in the "Preparation" section.

Rule #136: Hardware, aisle three.

While some malls *may* have a gun shop/sporting goods store somewhere on the premises (Or immediately outside, though still on the mall grounds), all malls *will* have some kind of hardware store or a store with a hardware department *somewhere* within its halls. In the event you can't escape and there isn't a place to find firearms, GET TO THESE PLACES IMMEDIATELY!!! Things like axes, hatchets, crowbars, hammers, screwdrivers, and nail guns are excellent zombie killing equipment and are likely the best things you can get your hands on in such dire circumstances and are also your best chance of survival in this situation. It may be a gauntlet getting to them, but, really, you don't have much of a choice. I could insert a joke about tools here, but, this is serious.

Rule #137: Kitchenware, aisle four.

Okay, here's your scenario: You can't escape, there aren't any gun/sporting good stores at your mall, and *Sears's* hardware department is jammed with zombies. What do you do? Easy: Run to *the other* kind of store *every mall* has: Cooking stores. Cooking stores are usually your best place to find meat tenderizers (The metallic ones are best; they're the sturdiest for our purposes), cleavers, rolling pins, butcher knives and, perhaps, frying pans, most of which would serve as excellent weapons to cave in zombie skulls (The frying pan is, admittedly… questionable). If you have no better option or you need some back-up weaponry just in case, *this* is the place to go.

Rule #138: Grab firearms where available.

As mentioned in the previous two rules (#136 & 137, respectively), *some* malls have sporting goods/gun stores on their premises, in some cases, just outside and still technically on said premises (Although, if there are legions of zombies outside, it may be way too far for you to reach safely). If you have the option of reaching these weapons and escape is, at least for the moment, unlikely (For argument's sake, let's say the doors are mobbed by zombie shoppers), *this* is definitely your best option for both offense and defense. As you navigate your way through the mall looking for whatever else you may need (Perhaps an exit) having a solid gun is, as discussed throughout this book, your best means of keeping the undead off of you, and, should they be blocking your escape, also your best way of clearing a path through them. Regardless of what you need them for, guns stand at the top of the *Zombie Killing Pyramid* © and, so long as you can get them, you SHOULD.

Zombie Killing Pyramid
(Accounting for "The Goldilocks Zone")

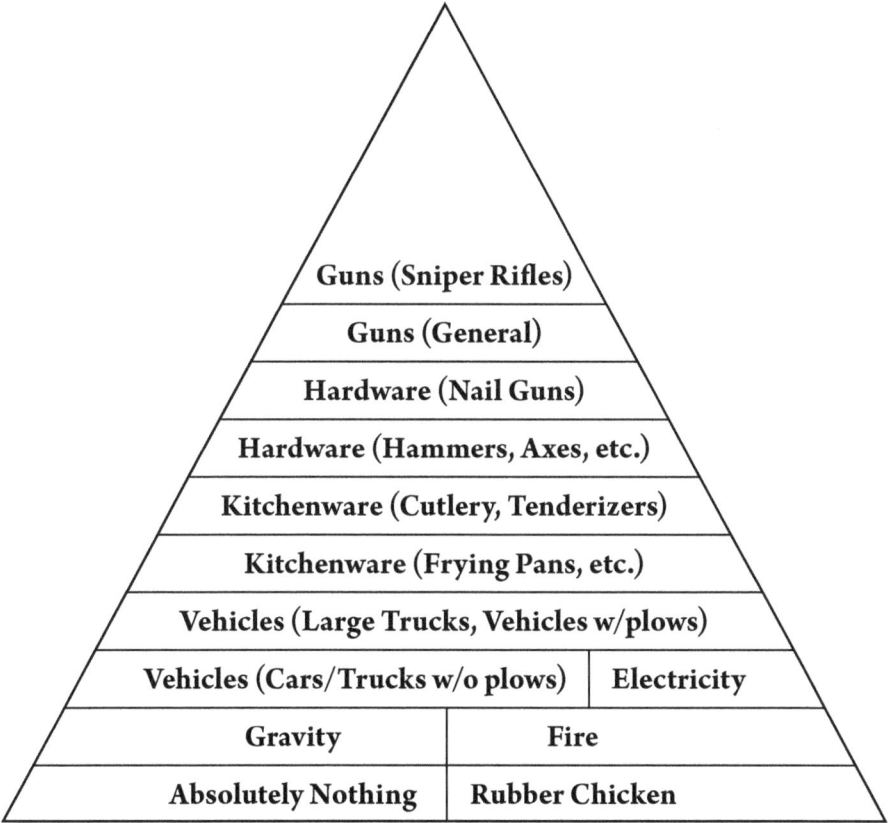

```
                    Guns (Sniper Rifles)
                     Guns (General)
                  Hardware (Nail Guns)
             Hardware (Hammers, Axes, etc.)
           Kitchenware (Cutlery, Tenderizers)
             Kitchenware (Frying Pans, etc.)
         Vehicles (Large Trucks, Vehicles w/plows)
      Vehicles (Cars/Trucks w/o plows) | Electricity
              Gravity          |          Fire
         Absolutely Nothing    |     Rubber Chicken
```

As the pyramid clearly indicates, guns are the best weapon you have against the undead, because of their ability to kill them relatively accurately from a distance (Note that "Sniper Rifles" sits atop the pyramid just for this reason). As we go further down, our weapons require you be closer or need more time to effectively kill zombies, but this should serve as a good reference for all your zombie killing needs.

Rule #139: DON'T plan on staying.

At first glance, this may seem like a no-brainer, you may look at this and say "Stay?! Who the @%&* would stay in a zombie-infested mall?!" And, if you happen to be asking this question, then good, it means you've been paying attention! But, absurd as this may seem, there may be some out there who think that if they clear out the zombies (Good luck doing that by yourself if there are no guns, by the way...), or keep them on a different floor (Again, good luck with that...) then The Mall may not be a bad place to hold up until the worst of Z-Day blows over. Those people would be wrong. Yes, *IF* (And that, by the way is an *EXTREMELY LONG* stretch for an "if"...) you were able to get rid of the zombies inside, or isolate them on an individual floor, then The Mall can serve as a reasonable place in the short term. However, survival is *NOT* just about the short term, The Mall's food and water supplies, especially if the power is lost, will only last for so long, and, assuming that you had the means to keep the rest of the zombies out of your new sanctuary, well, you know how this story ends: Eventually the presence of a few zombies attracts a few more, and a few more, *AND A FEW **MORE***. Eventually, our brave survivor finds himself trapped in what is quickly becoming a gilded prison; he has all of these marvelous things at his disposal, but his means of escape is slowly being cut off, his food is dwindling from consumption or decay and he is painfully aware that his water supply is limited and will eventually run out: He is doomed to a slow, torturous death...and he *knows it* (We aren't even going to get into the possibility of raiders disrupting his prison and letting the zombies *IN*...). Unless you are **COMPLETELY, 100%, UNABLE TO ESCAPE, staying in The Mall SHOULD NOT BE AN OPTION!!!! PERIOD!!!!**

Rule #140: Avoid parking garages whenever possible.

Okay, you're in trouble: Most of the exits are choked with zombies. More are coming. You need out…now. Where do you go? Do you brave the host of corpses at the door? Do you try drawing them away and lose them later? Do you look for a zombie-free exit? Or…do you try to escape via the dark, enclosed, wreckage clogged parking garage? If, *and ONLY IF* the previous options are impossible, should you consider *this* at all. Why?! Simple, most mall doors are windowed; you can see the zombies coming. If they're inside, you *should* have a good idea where they are. *The garage*, however, is perilously dark (Or perilously bright, see Rule #109), dangerously high (If you must jump off of it, a real possibility) *and,* especially if it's still filled with cars, *extremely tight.* The garage will be a huge wild card, where you'll be totally blind to what the next threat is (One zombie, ten…*a hundred*) or *where* it's coming from. Sure, there's a shot it's clear, but, can you *afford* to get halfway through the garage, only to find a mob of zombies awaiting you? No…you can't.

Rule #141: Keep them where you can see them.

Again, if The Mall has become largely infested with (Or surrounded by) zombies, and you haven't gotten out, you... *should* start thinking about it...seriously. With this in mind, you're gonna want to be sure that you have as many of the zombies where you can see them as possible. If at all possible, try luring the zombies away from your preferred exits. Also, as long as it's safe to do so, search The Mall as best as possible: Check every possible hiding spot anyone may have taken at the onset of the outbreak, they may have hidden there after being bitten and turned since, carefully check every possible escape you may have and make sure there are no surprises. The last thing you want is to go out an exit, only to find every zombie on the premises waiting for you. Trust me; this will be important for the next rule.

Rule #142: Look for staff entrances.

This is tricky. If you wait too long to flee, you may have tons of ghouls waiting for you at every mall entrance. *However,* unlike the regular entrances to The Mall, the employee entrances are almost always incapable of being opened from outside or without a key (Which it's highly unlikely *any* zombie can use), meaning that zombies won't even REALIZE that a person *can* exit from there, and probably won't bother hanging around it. If you move quickly (i.e. *BEFORE* the whole place is surrounded by zombies), you can make a break for the outside, preferably near your car. Do take precautions to have a quick...*very* quick, once over of the terrain, so that, if you *weren't* following Rule #141 ("Keep them where you can see them") and didn't fool all the zombies into going to an exit far from the service entrance you're planning on escaping from, you can see how many (If any) ghouls are near your port of escape. If you've moved fast enough, you can burst through the door and make a break for the outside before things get too bad. If not...um...nice knowing you.

Rule #143: It's a long way down. Use it to your advantage.

Most malls today have at least two floors, some, especially in major cities, may have three or more. Now, think about those extra floors in your local mall. Can you picture them? Good. Now, ask yourself: "Do I feel comfortable *jumping* from this floor down to the ground?" If the answer is no (As it *should be*) then, congratulations, you've just found a "Last ditch" weapon you can use on zombies: Gravity. I'm sure those who've been paying attention are saying "Wait, wasn't gravity at *the bottom* of the *Zombie Killing Pyramid©?*" And, they're right: Gravity should *only* be used when *no other means of offense* is available. Why? Easy, utilizing gravity requires you to either: a) Get close to zombies and knock them to the floor below (Hopefully killing or at least crippling them) or b) Have a system of knocking them over from a distance (Yeah…right), neither are good prospects. However, if you lack other weapons, and doing so does *not* get you swarmed by zombies, then by all means, start tossing them over the railing and down to the floor! Just don't get bitten…

Rule #144: Don't go into places you don't know your way out of.

Having worked at a mall I can clue you into something you may not know: The part of The Mall you shop in is only *a fraction* of the actual building itself. Behind the stores, behind everything is a shadow world, and underworld, where the trash gets thrown out and where the merchandise gets delivered: The Mall's "World within the World". With it being almost completely separated from the shopping arcades and limited access to the outside world, you'd think it's an ideal place to hide from the undead. But, much like *staying* in The Mall, you'd be *WRONG*. Unless you've worked down there, strolling into The Mall's underworld is *worse* than adventuring into the garage, as you don't know if, where, or how many zombies roam those dark creepy halls or where to go should you meet them! Plus, The Mall underground is surprisingly vast and dark and, unlike The Mall itself, has no windows to the outside. For all you know, you could open a garage door to dozens of zombies, because you have no idea what's on the other side!! So, unless you have a map of the mall's inner workings handy, DO NOT go down in there... you may never find your way out alive...

Train Rules

Trains, like malls, are self-contained environments which present their own special set of challenges, which we will discuss in this section. Included are how to deal with the confines, lack of supplies, and of course...the fact that its moving at least 30 MPH on average and crashing could kill you <u>before</u> a single zombie even lays a hand on you. So, while I hope you don't find yourself in such a vehicle when Z-Day hits (Which is the scenario we're looking at, here), here is some help should you be one of the poor bastards who <u>DO</u>. Good luck.

Rule #145: <u>STOP...THE...TRAIN!</u>

If you find yourself trapped on a moving train, you only have a limited amount of time before the train either derails or crashes, and either way, your train has now become your coffin. To prevent this, you need to make every effort possible to stop it before that happens. In some cases, this may only require you to bust down the door to the conductor's cockpit and tell the conductor to hit the brakes; in others, this may force you to run a gauntlet from one end of the train to the other, dodging and fighting off zombies as best as possible, only to kill the zombified conductor and stop the train yourself. Either way, should you *not* do that, your prospects for survival are dangerously low (Although, should this be your only option, there *are* alternatives, which we'll discuss soon).

Rule #146: Find something...ANYTHING!!

Let's face it, trains are...trains. They're not tanks, fire trucks or police cars: They do *NOT* have weapons intended to be accessed by their crews because, frankly, when would they need them? Of course, on Z-Day, this is a **BIG** problem. In a worst-case scenario, you'll find yourself on a *packed* train, filled either with zombies or a panicking mob slowly *becoming* zombies; fighting either barehanded is *suicide*. So, you need to do whatever possible to arm yourself with something to both keep you at arm's length of the zombies and put them down. I'll bet you're wondering "How the Hell am I supposed to arm myself when there are *no WEAPONS* on the damned train?!"... well...*that* is indeed a good question, and while weapons may be scarce (Or non-existent) there may be ways for you defend yourself: Some trains have storage compartments on the passenger cars for the purpose of storing various tools and almost (If not all) trains have fire extinguishers. It may not be a shotgun, but...it's better than nothing.

Rule #147: Cut yourself off from the disease.

As discussed earlier, depending on where you are, attempting to stop the train may be an insurmountable gauntlet of cramped, zombie congested cars whilst you're likely unarmed (As we've just discussed). If this is the case you find yourself in, I have good news: You *DO* have an alternative!! If you can push you way to the end of the train (This may be easier or more difficult depending on what city/train line you find yourself on; Chicago, for example, allows passengers to freely travel between cars) there's a chance you'll have access to the latches which hold one car to the next, if you can successfully detach them, you only have to survive long enough for it to either drift to a stop, or slow down to a speed which will make it safe for you to jump out and escape. It sure as Hell beats having to make that nightmarish gauntlet through the rest of the damned train.

> Side Note: While following this rule may allow you to escape the train without the risk of making your way through the rest of it, it does come with its own potential complications, that being: You have no idea what may happen to the rest of the train once you're out of it. It's entirely possible it could derail a few hundred yards away and strike a gas main leading to a fireball which will almost certainly make its way towards you (This is far more likely if you happen to be on a subway as opposed to an overland train). Should this happen, you need to run as fast and as hard as possible in the opposite direction, both to avoid any potential disasters stemming from the train's possible derailment as well as any zombies possibly roaming around in the dark train tunnels (A la Rule #124, "Avoid train tunnels").

Rule #148: Be prepared for a fight.

While all the other previously mentioned areas which have their own specific rules (Cities, Suburbs, Malls) one thing they all have in common is open space, even if it may seem relatively small while you're in them, compared to the amount of space you'll have in the train (Even in a *best* case scenario, never mind a worst case) it's like having free reign over a cornfield!! This is because, no matter what kind of train or where it is, trains are *incredibly* tight (Again, even in the best of circumstances), and the more people, living or undead, that occupy it, the worse it becomes. The reason for the reiteration of what I'm sure is obvious to you is this: If you think you can just dodge around all the zombies you'll encounter, **THINK AGAIN!!** Sooner or later, you'll *HAVE TO* fight them! Now, as mentioned in Rule #146 ("Find something… ANYTHING"), this may prove difficult, as your choice of weaponry is likely very limited. Regardless, you really have no choice, if you want to live, you'll have to be ready to fight the undead sooner or later…but preferably later.

Rule #149: Remember The Spartans.

...The Spartans...like in *300?* Exactly. The reason why people the world over are taught about the battle of Thermopylae (That's the name of the battle for those who don't know/ remember) in history class is for two reasons: One, it's a defining moment of Western Civilization; Two, it shows how a smaller, but more determined force was able to hold back (And nearly defeat) a much larger army using clever strategy and forcing their enemy to fall into that strategy. How does this apply to trains? Easy, trains, with their naturally confined spaces, have several natural chokepoints which can help you neutralize the zombies' superior numbers. So long as you've been able to find some sort of weapon (Likely a fire extinguisher – it's cumbersome but will have to do for our circumstances), you can use one of these chokepoints, preferably the space between cars or the end of an aisle of seats (If they're facing the same direction as the train), to keep your fight with the undead one-on-one. If you can keep to this tactic, you might...correction...*will* have a much better chance of surviving your fight with them than you would trying to fight them as an ever more tightly encircling mob. Whether you want to kick them in the chest out of the train is entirely up to you.

Rule #150: When all else fails...JUMP!!!!!

This rule, as one might gather from its name, is something of a last resort, only to be used if you have no other recourse. If you can't reach the conductor's cockpit, can't separate the cars, **AND** find that you have *absolutely* no means of fighting the undead (Which are likely encroaching upon you if you need to consider this at all), then you may have no choice but find some opening, be it a window or door, and jump out of the train. If the train is flying at some thirty-forty miles an hour (If you were able to slow down the train even slightly, then this isn't nearly as bad of an issue), this is definitely a dangerous prospect, especially if you're not skilled in the fine art of "Tuck and Roll". However, if you're really considering this, then you are *already* out of options and the alternative... is becoming a zombie. When faced with that choice, it really isn't a choice at all. ...Happy landings!

Rule #151: Keep them on one side of you.

This would also work as a general rule, but works especially well here. With trains being rather linear by design, doing this is *slightly* easier than it would be in the other specific locations we've already discussed. Now, how you do this and to what end is entirely up to you; whether you intend on using Rule #149 ("Remember the Spartans") and fighting them or using Rule #147 ("Cut yourself off...") and running from them, the important thing is: It *MUST* be done. If not, with the tight confines of a train, it's *perilously easy* for the undead to surround you and then, it's too late. A fast moving person will at least attempt to get to one end of their car (If it's really crowded, try pushing through for the end with the least amount of screaming coming from it, there are likely less zombies over there), so as to have no way for the zombies to get behind/in front of them as they attempt to fight/escape. Should there be a few zombies confusedly staggering around, *KILL THEM* **IMMEDIATELY,** as you can't afford having more gather before you're ready to fight/escape, in fact, the need to kill these ones staggering around can *NOT* be overstated. Once those stragglers are dealt with, you should have a few precious seconds to plan your next move and whether fighting them or running from them is better for you. Whatever you pick, the important thing is to stick with the rule, *DON'T* run into a mob of zombies and *DON'T* get yourself into a circumstance where they can surround you (This isn't to say *stop* fighting them, but don't jump into the middle of them to fight them, that's just dumb). One advantage: Should you be running, (So long as you're sticking to the rule) if there are more zombies in the next car...at least they're all on one side of you...now get crackin'!

Rural/Country Rules

The country, with its wide open spaces and sparse population has both its own benefits and detriments. As with the other locations discussed here, we're under the assumption that you are completely unprepared for what Z-Day will entail. These rules are meant to help either exploit or confront the different conditions found in these places...y'all.

Rule #152: When you find shelter, TAKE IT!!!

In the country, there may be miles (In some places, *many* miles) between one house and the next and, keep in mind, you *are* unprepared: You have no food, no water, no weapons. Therefore, it would behoove the smart survivor to take advantage of this shelter should you be lucky enough to find some. Why? Because eventually, it's gonna get dark. Previously, we'd gone over (Rule #105, "Don't go out at night", to be exact) the dangers present in wandering around at night: In the darkness and quiet of night, you can very easily attract (Or just plain stumble into) roaming zombies. So, rather than blunder into certain doom, take refuge for the night in the nearest shelter you find the moment nightfall draws near. Trust me; you'll thank me the next morning.

Rule #153: The comforts of home.

Homes in the country may or may not be quite as furnished as their counterparts in the suburbs, but, because of the nature of life in the country, may possess things homes in the suburbs may not (Side Note: *May.* This isn't to say that such things *couldn't* be found in the suburbs) otherwise find in said suburbs: Like axes, pitchforks, pickaxes, fireplace pokers, etc. Of course, this also applies to things like backpacks, gym bags, food, water, and whatever else you find that's useful. Should you find such things, especially weapons, GRAB'EM! They *might* become useful soon…I don't know, maybe.

Rule #154: Take out the rubbish.

As mentioned earlier in Rule #152 ("When you find shelter, TAKE IT!!"), out here, shelter is precious, and it is up to you to ensure that it's safe for you to stay in (The last thing you need is to try and get some sleep only to find there are *already* occupants inside...*undead ones*). In other words, you need to scour your new home and make sure there are *no* zombies roaming around, and should there be, you need to use whatever means you have to kill the damned thing(s) before it invites *you* to join it. This is where Rule #153 ("The comforts of home") can come in handy. Should you be adhering to it, you probably already have some kind of weaponry for making sure that the zombie(s) in question never get the chance to make said invitation formal.

> Side Note: Try to avoid using guns when dealing with any lingering zombies as best as possible. Out here, the relative emptiness of your surroundings can make gunshots **REALLY** *noticeable* and your goal at this point to *get rid of* the zombies, not draw more to you.

Rule #155: Need to bear arms.

You've heard me go on and on about the need to have guns on Z-Day; they make killing zombie far easier, be it from a distance or in close quarters, and surviving Z-Day without them, while not impossible, is a helluva lot tougher. However, if you're in the country on Z-Day, CONGRATULATIONS!! People in the country are often armed for both hunting (For food and sport) and protection (Farmers or ranchers need to keep their livestock safe from wolves, coyotes and mountain lions, which *could* be zombified too, don't forget). This means there's a good chance that whatever shelter you find has some kind of firearm within it! If the place is home to zombies, you may have to settle with one of the items mentioned in Rule #154 ("Take out the rubbish"), before you explore for said firearms. But, regardless, the moment there are no zombies in the vicinity (Not necessarily assuming you cleaned the place up entirely, but enough to search the main floor), you should search high and low for any guns and hang onto them; they're gonna save your life someday...

Rule #156: Don't draw attention to yourself.

Remember how I told you that houses in the country can be *very far* from one another? Yeah, this means that you do *NOT* want to do **_anything_** that might compromise that sanctuary (You're gonna have to sleep here for a night at least, most likely) which means the following: Don't shoot anything unless you have to (See the Side Note for Rule #154, "Take out the rubbish" for more on this topic), if you're gonna barricade anything, do it fast and do whatever you can to *be quiet* about it, shut off all the lights, and hide, preferably in a drawstring attic (Which we will discuss later). If you don't follow this (Or maybe even if you do, you don't know how perceptive they may be...), it may not be long before the zombies start knocking on your door and eventually surrounding the house (And no, they're not selling cookies). While they may still attempt to come in, there's no reason to advertise.

Rule #157: Attics: First choice.

Even if you've stayed quiet as a dead mouse, it is *still possible* that the undead may be drawn to your location (Again, it's up to you to find out just how smart they are – Rule #28, "Know your enemy"). This circumstance may force you to seek refuge somewhere else within the house; the ideal location for which being the attic. *Wait...the attic?* Yes, the attic. *Why?* Well first, most attics have windows, so, in the event the undead *do* break in and find their way to the attic, you have a means of escape which *won't* lead you directly to the (Likely) swarming mass of zombies surrounding your would-be sanctuary (Jumping from the roof *can* give you a few precious yards of separation between yourself and the undead). Better still, if the attic is accessible via a drawstring ladder, CONGRATULATIONS!! So long as you pull the string in after getting into the attic (Don't be a dumbass and leave it dangling!!), the zombies will have almost *no way* of getting to you (They're almost certainly not smart enough to use hammers...or ladders for that matter), so you can just wait them out until they stumble upon easier prey! But wait, *THERE'S MORE!!* Should the attic be accessible to the zombies, the stairwell makes for a great funnel to counter the zombies' superior numbers (For details, see Rule #149, "Remember the Spartans")! So basically, a decent attic is a win-win situation.

Rule #158: Basements: Last resort.

For all the benefits the attic can provide, the basement is, often times, the complete opposite. Case in point: The attic, so long as it gives you roof access (Even if it doesn't, the wood from the roof is easier to break through than the concrete and cinderblocks of the basement) gives you much better chances of keeping your distance from the zombies. *The basement,* on the other hand, has, (At best) doors which lead *directly* to where the zombies are hungrily waiting for you! This *isn't* to say it doesn't have its upsides (The bottleneck effect we discussed earlier also happens with the basement, too). But, just a reminder, the above scenario -- You know, where your only door leads you straight to the zombies – is the **best-case scenario**. Yeah, you don't wanna know what the worst-case scenario is like: Imagine you're trapped within concrete or cinder block walls, with the *only staircase* leading out clogged with zombies. If you can picture that, you've got a good idea of what the worst case scenario looks like…

Rule #159: No shelter? Stick to the woods.

One advantage to being in the country on Z-Day is that you have lots of wild terrain far from any large (Relatively) groups of people. If you *can't* find shelter on Z-Day, the woods may make a good hiding place, at least until you find a zombie-free building. *Wait...the woods?* Yes. The woods, unlike farmland, has tons of natural security systems to use: Rocks and trees to slow zombies down, sticks and leaves to warn you they're coming, and lots of foliage and debris (Along with rocks and trees) to hide you from them. While I bet you think I'm crazy for suggesting it, think about this: Farmland gives you NO protection. Yes, it may take a while to find you, but...so what? It won't take much for one (Maybe several) zombie(s) to push their way through a cornfield and find you, as corn, unlike trees, is relative easy for a person to push through. Also, as farm crops are arranged in rows, the moment a zombie makes his way into your row and *sees YOU*, there is absolutely nothing to stop him from strolling over and having you for supper with a side of his favorite veggies.

Hospital Rules

<u>These</u> are important. No place is less safe to be in on Z-Day than a hospital (Except for a plane, but...that's almost a write-off), as no place is more likely to see a massive influx of soon-to-be zombies in such a short span of time. As the situation outside deteriorates, more "injured" people come in, they'll zombify, bite doctors and nurses, and soon you'll have zombies, zombie doctors and zombie nurses. So, as with our location specific rules, we're going to assume the absolute worst-case scenario: You are an (Unprepared) patient at your local hospital, itself within a city, when Z-Day hits. It should also be noted that several of the rules discussing high-rise buildings from the city rule section should also be thought to apply here as well, in case your particular hospital has three or more floors. If you didn't have a problem with hospitals <u>before</u>, you're going to have one <u>now.</u>

Rule #160: GET UP!!!!

If you find yourself lying in a hospital (Frankly *any* hospital is bad on Z-Day, pick your favorite) on Z-Day, you're obviously *not* in the best of shape, if you were, you probably wouldn't be at the hospital in the first place...that being said, unless you're totally paralyzed, you *MUST* move!! Even if it's difficult, even if it's painful, even if it's *slow*, moving forward *at all* is light-years better than just lying there waiting for a zombified doctor to rip your jugular out! Getting up off your ass and making for the exit is the first step in the road to recovery, and trust me, it's gonna be a bumpy one...

Rule #161: Find some shoes.

This rule may seem absurd, but frankly, God only knows *when* Z-Day will hit. Depending on what time of year it is, (And it should be noted the tile floors of most hospitals *are not* heated) should you escape, you may find yourself wandering around *barefoot **in a foot of snow!!*** In that case, you'll die of hypothermia long before a zombie can even lay a hand on you! Never mind that having shoes provides a much needed barrier between you and the teeth of any crawling zombies intent on eating your feet (And, should you realize that crushing/stomping/punting a zombie's head is a useful way to get rid of it, it helps to do so with ***SHOES ON!!!!***). Hopefully, the hospital will have been kind enough to leave *your* shoes next to your bed. If not, you may have to settle with those of someone else either in your room or in another. While we're on this topic, you may need to grab some clothes, too.

Rule #162: Emergency supplies.

Normally, **_I WOULD NOT SUGGEST THIS, EVER_**.
However, *this **is*** an emergency: You just got out of your hospital
bed, you hear ghouls groaning from somewhere behind your
door. This is…BAD. You don't know what's waiting for you
outside; those groans could just be coming from zombies
sealed behind a door at the end of the hall…or it could be
from an undead mob *just outside **your** door*!! Either way, you
need *something* to fight them with until you get real weapons,
and, being in a hospital, the nearest source is the one thing
you'd normally do everything to avoid (And rightly so): The
used needle box. Since you need weapons *yesterday*, the best
thing to do is dump the box on the floor (Reaching in to grab
them is just plain **DUMB**, *DON'T DO IT!!*) grab as many as
you'll think you'll need **_BY THE HANDLE_** and tie them to
yourself (The belt loop of your pants is a good place, should
you have them) so that, should zombies, in fact, *be* waiting
for you, you can jab needles in their heads and then run like
Hell in the other direction.

Rule #163: Find the supply closet.

In most places, this is just a tiny space filled with ink, pens, staplers, etc. *In a hospital*, however, this place will likely have things much more necessary for your escape: Scalpels, *clean* syringes, surgical knives and scissors, all things that will be tremendously helpful in killing zombies. What's more, each floor is likely to have one, so you *shouldn't* be too far from one no matter where you are (This depends on the layout of the hospital, but having such supplies far from where they're needed is perilously impractical and hospitals do what they can to *stop people from dying,* so they'll likely have at least one on each floor to keep the staff supplied in case of emergencies). Remember to stock up, you don't know how many zombies will be between here and the next one.

> Side Note: Be prepared to kick in doors. Hospitals will likely have these doors locked and trying to search for keys may be time-consuming or involve dealing with zombies. So, as long as the zombies aren't encroaching on you, kick in that door, grab your arsenal and get the Hell out of there!!

Rule #164: Find the nearest operating room.

Operating rooms, most hospitals have them. Normally, they're where a master surgeon carves into your body to remove things that don't belong there. That's...*normally,* Z-Day, of course, is *not* normal. On Z-Day, operating rooms may as well be called armories, as the many surgical blades likely left behind in the panic will be a treasure trove of weapons for you to kill zombies with, and, being *surgical tools,* they'll prove extremely sharp and quite deadly. You will, however, be required to dispatch or elude (Dispatching is better) any zombies that may occupy the room. Hopefully, all the surgeons panicked and hightailed it before they were infected.

> Side Note: Again, these being *surgical tools,* they will prove **incredibly sharp**, sharper likely than anything you've ever used before. So, be careful not to slice yourself up either jamming said tools (Scalpels, for example) into *or* prying them out of the heads of zombies, doing so leaves you open to contamination and, eventually, zombification, should their blood get into any fresh (And likely deep) cuts you may give yourself mishandling such sharp utensils. No point in getting turned into a zombie because of sheer dumb carelessness.

Rule #16: "Shocking. Positively shocking."

One advantage of being in a hospital on Z-Day which you may not realize: Hospitals are veritable arsenals. They contain needles, scalpels, scissors, and knives (As mentioned previously), nevermind emergency tools like axes and fire extinguishers. But perhaps the best weapon is one you may overlook... *The Defibrillator.* Defibrillators are devices used by ER doctors to revive potentially dying patients by jolting the heart with electricity. Normally, these are big and cumbersome, but, there *are* portable ones, which, when the electrodes are placed on either side of a zombie's head, can basically fry the brain, making it a very lethal weapon which you can use against zombies. Even without juice, the electrodes are often relatively heavy and can serve as hammers, crushing skulls with relative ease. Things may have just gotten *a little bit* easier...

(And, yes, that quote was from the classic *James Bond* movie, *Goldfinger.* For our purposes, imagine that being spoken in your *best* Sean Connery accent.)

Rule #166: Avoid the emergency entrance unless absolutely necessary.

This is fairly simple: The emergency entrance of a hospital is, obviously, where the majority of grievously injured people would go during a disaster, and there is no bigger disaster than Z-Day. This means that, in a relatively short amount of time, this portion of the hospital will likely become the epicenter of zombie activity, and therefore, unless you are otherwise certain it is free of zombies (Or you have ***ABSOLUTELY NO OTHER CHOICE***) ***AVOID*** this area as best as humanly possible!!!

Rule #167: Avoid the morgue, too, while you're at it.

Normally, most (Living) visitors to the hospital do *not* visit the morgue, for obvious reasons. On Z-Day, however, you may think to go there, as the morgue is often close to an exit (For the purpose of delivering corpses). Of course, the nature of both Z-Day and the morgue means that, like the emergency entrance, it will soon become a nexus of recently *reanimated* corpses, and likely be too dangerous to be worth attempting an escape from. You'd best try to find a less populated area to escape through, unless this is your **ONLY** option.

> Side Note: There is the possibility that your only escape options are the ones most likely to have the largest population of undead in/near them: The emergency exit or the morgue, a dubious prospect either way. While there is likely to be some difficulty picking, the best advice I have is: Do whatever you can to scout these areas, so long as it's viable to do so. Whichever has the least (Or most advantageously dispersed) zombies both inside and outside of these areas should be the exit you attempt to escape from. While it's almost guaranteed that you'll run into zombies either way, you'll want to deal with as few or at least as scattered a group of zombies as possible.

Hospital Rules, Sub Section: Laboratory Rules

This may seem out of place, but think about it: Have you seen a zombie before? Have you ever heard of anyone else seeing a zombie before? The answer to those is no. This is because zombies are unnatural and, should you need to adhere to this rulebook at all, it's probably because someone did something they were not supposed to in a lab. On Z-Day, you have no knowledge of where you may take refuge and what's more, you have no idea where you might stumble onto a laboratory, but a hospital is just as likely (If not a little more) to be the place where you may find yourself in one. Now for these rules, we're not necessarily assuming that Z-Day has hit. Maybe, by following these rules, we can avoid the whole damned thing altogether.

Rule #168: Leave the animals ALONE!!!!!

This is for all you "animal people" out there. Should you, for any reason, be in a laboratory (Research hospital, college, government facility, whatever) *do not...**FOR ANY REASON**...release...ANY...**ANIMALS!!!!***

I'm sure you find the state of the animals simply *being* caged cruel but, I *IMPLORE YOU, FOR THE LOVE OF GOD...* just leave them alone.

"But, they don't belong in cages!" you say.

Whether or not this is true, think of this: First, if they are any sort of primate (Often used to test something that could later be used on humans), they probably *DON'T* belong in your area; they're an invasive species and mean bad news for everything local: Plants, animals, everything. Second, if the experiments are of an infectious nature, if you let them out, they <u>WILL</u> infect any other animals they come into contact with. Third, animals are not necessarily very good at distinguishing one human from another, and even if they are, when they're scared, injured or angry (Which, considering their circumstances, is highly probable) they're likely to lash out at the first thing they get a chance to lash out at, which in this case, is YOU. Finally (And *this* is the important one), do you *know* what these animals were experimented on *with?!*

.... I'm waiting for an answer.

...No? Okay. This means, for all you know, they could contain *zombie virus*. Think about this for a minute. Now, put together what we just mentioned. ...If you have half a brain, it just hit you: If you let these things *out*, first, they will attack (And *zombify*) *you*. Then, they'll likely infect anyone around you. Lastly (As this may be most important to you), they will likely infect *EVERY* **OTHER** *ANIMAL THEY COME IN CONTACT WITH, WHICH WILL INFECT EVERYTHING ELSE!!* So basically, I'm telling you that if you go monkeying around with animals you do not know, being experimented on with God only knows what, then *You* (Yes, **_You_**) will have initiated **Z-Day**. ***Congratulations!!*** ...You are a douche...you douche.

Rule #169: Don't listen to the scientist who says "We need it ALIVE."

Remember what I said way back in Rule #9 ("There is NO CURE") about trying to find a cure in a *secure research hospital*? If, **AND _ONLY_ IF** *that* is your base and **ONLY IF** the person suggesting this is, in fact, a *real* scientist (No amateur Frankensteins, please) *skilled in disease control*, should the above notion even be *remotely* entertained. Otherwise, you are in *SERIOUS TROUBLE.*

Side Note: Take note that *securely* sealing up *a zombie* (Singular, two or more is begging for the above *SERIOUS TROUBLE*) *can* assist with Rule #28, "Know your enemy". *BUT, and I _CAN NOT_ stress this ENOUGH, THE SECOND you've learned everything about how intelligent/ strong/tough the undead are, VERY CAREFULLY, _DESTROY IT!!!_ Keeping active zombies around for any longer is EXTREMELY DANGEROUS! And do not let some amateur try to put down this zombie! You need someone skilled in firearms (Preferably shotguns) waiting to shoot it. IF YOU LACK A TRULY SECURE PLACE for the zombie and ALSO LACK A PERSON SKILLED IN KILLING GHOULS AND A GOOD WEAPON, DO _NOT_ DO THIS!! Only under these VERY SPECIFIC CIRCUMSTANCES should any such act be attempted.*

Rule #170: Keep a close eye on the scientist who says "We need it ALIVE."

As mentioned in the last rule, such an idea should only be entertained under *VERY* specific circumstances. That said, should you be lucky enough to find yourself in such circumstances, and you *DO* happen to have a capable scientist who feels they can learn something useful from studying zombies, **NEVER LET THEM OUT OF YOUR SIGHT!** It's very easy for people in that field, the study of zombies and their...*practical* uses, to become *obsessed* with the potential to be found *in* them, and, in so doing, have a "Reserved Freak-out", where, while they may not be panicky, violent, or suicidal, they may be crossing into dangerous territory, where they value the existence of *zombies* over that of *the living*.

Come to think of it, this may be *why* you're dealing with zombies in the first place...hmm...

City/Suburb Rules, Sub Section: Apartment Rules

Apartments are a convenient way for lots of people to live in one building. Normally, they are a fine way to live... normally. But, on Z-Day, with multiple stories, elevators (Possibly), lack of windows (Or windows that can't open), inability to see what's outside your door and limited access points, they can quickly become deathtraps, and soon, zombie recruiting stations. So, in the hopes of helping up your chances of escaping your apartment alive, I've taken the liberty of setting down a few rules to help you have a plan, should Z-Day catch you by surprise whilst in an apartment. I should mention, I live in an apartment. So trust me...I've put thought into these...a lot.

Rule #171: Lock the door.

At first glance, this may seem counterproductive: You obviously *want* to get out as quickly as possible. However, after careful consideration, I've concluded this is actually the *first* thing you should do, for one simple reason: You likely have *no idea* what's waiting for you outside, and you'll need a minute to get your bearings (Which we discuss next), the *last* thing you want is for zombies to just push open your door and stroll in, do you?

No, you don't.

So, *anything* you can do to slow them down for a few precious minutes, especially where it will only *take you a few seconds*, you *should* do. Besides, it's not like they can pick locks.

Rule #172: Grab any weapons you can find.

This is what I meant earlier by "Get your bearings", and how well you're able to do it really depends on you. If you have a gun, great, go grab it and whatever ammo you can carry, you're gonna need it. If not, grab whatever is handy: Baseball bat, golf club, rolling pin, meat cleaver, meat tenderizer, butcher knife, cast iron frying pan, a hammer, a long screwdriver, sharp knives, a fireplace poker, a long, sturdy pair of scissors... **WHATEVER** makes for a viable weapon(s) against zombies; the longer, the better (Remember Rule #24, "...The Goldilocks Zone"), the more durable the better, as you may have a long hard fight on your hands. Once you're armed, you can now start trying to make your way out. Trust me, you'll have *something* worth using, you have to (I honestly can't imagine someone not having at least *one* of the items mentioned above). You don't wanna be trying to make it out empty-handed...you **won't** get far.

Rule #173: Look before you leap.

Okay, you're armed…now what? First, if you have a peephole, scope it out *carefully* (You don't want any zombies outside possibly getting wise to any change in light coming from said peephole if you can avoid it, or worse, seeing a tiny human face staring back at them). If you can't see any, press your ear against the door or near the doorstop and check if you can hear them coming (You know, groans, footsteps perhaps proceeded by the screams of…well…*your neighbors*, and the sounds of ripping flesh). If you can't see or hear them, sniff… can you smell dead bodies nearby (You won't be able to miss it)? If not, then *now* is your time to make a break for the hallway, the *first* step in your treacherous escape.

> Side Note: Do what you can to stymie any reactions you may have to seeing, hearing or *smelling* the undead. If they are not aware of your presence *before*, the sudden sound of a scream…or sudden smell of vomit, is sure to alert them to you *after*.

Rule #174: The likeliest exit of least resistance.

The reason this rule is *not* "The exit closest to your vehicle" is because, right now, your *first* priority is just to **get out of the damned building!** With you being *in the building* and your car being *outside*...it might as well be on **Mars**. *The main entrance* will likely **flood** with zombies, and unfortunately, is likely where most of your neighbors are going to *try* to escape. Their success will be...*limited* at best (Think back to Rule #119, "Don't follow the crowd"). With this in mind, your goal is to find the exit *less traveled*, which is likely to have *less* zombies near it. Now, unless the exit is totally overrun by more zombies than you think you can handle, get ready to fight your way out (This is *why* you spent that time looking for weapons, remember), as going back to find another exit is probably going to get you into *more* fights with *more* zombies that are *nowhere near an exit*, so just stick with what you've got and fight your way out. *If* the exit you've found has way more than you think you can take on by yourself, then (And **_only_** then) should you backtrack to find another exit.

Rule #175: Take a moment to look behind you.

Imagine this: You've just come out your door. You look down the stairs and see zombies hovering down below; they don't see you. You quickly sneak across the floor and down the stairs on the opposite side, passing the remaining three apartments on your floor. You carefully make your way down the stairs, ensuring the zombies don't see you. While you keep your eyes on the zombies at the stairs ready to run if they notice you, you suddenly crash face-first to the floor. You glance back and all you see is a gaunt face lower itself toward you, its gaping maw made even more grisly by the large chunk torn from its left cheek. You are about to be bitten by a zombie.

Now, how the Hell did *this* happen? Did you notice anything in that scenario? ...No? Well, I'll tell you: You strolled past the other three apartments on your floor and *assumed* that everything was fine. **Bad move.** In this situation, even if there aren't zombies on the floor or roaming the halls, that by no means guarantees safety. Remember, there are other apartments all around you, for all you know, the occupants of each of those apartments were already infected *before the zombies even arrived* and have just turned now that they're here. **You have to assume** that each apartment houses *at least one* zombie and at anytime, they could see you, hear you, smell you and without even knowing it, you could be leading a parade of zombies. So, whenever you get a chance, take a second to look back and make sure there are no zombies sneaking up behind you, that extra second could mean the difference between a relatively clean getaway and a one way ticket to Hell you never saw coming.

Rule #176: Use your environment to your advantage.

How you follow this rule really depends on the layout of your apartment building. However, I will give you a couple examples to go by:

1) Narrow stairways and halls.

    If your building is like mine, the stairs connect directly to the hallway, with no doors separating them, this helps make them considerably narrow. As the zombies ascend the stairs, kick the lead one in the chest or somewhere else high on their center of gravity. Hopefully, this will cause them to fall back and topple the others behind them. In the halls, if they're narrow, much like in Rule #149 ("Remember The Spartans"), you can use them to effectively negate the zombies' numbers by forcing them to come at you one at a time.

2) High stairs and windows.

    We saw this earlier in Rule #143 ("It's a long way down…"), and the principal is the same. The stairs of most apartment buildings are made of concrete or steel, and neither are things you want to fall on, so….why not make *the zombies* fall on them instead?! The taller your apartment building is, the more effective this becomes, as the increased velocity combined with the hard surfaces they're likely to land on, will make the chances of them suffering zombie-killing injuries fairly high (Even if the fall doesn't kill them, they will likely be easy prey should you see them again). Furthermore, depending on how high it is, their landing may also cripple or destroy any of their cohorts waiting for them at the bottom of the stairs.

Rule #177: Fire escapes are for more than just fires.

I should begin by saying...duh. If you're in a building with a fire escape (So long as you trust it), **USE IT!** Fire escapes are *designed* to let you get to the ground while avoiding whatever plagues the building, in this case, *zombies*. They *do* have problems, though: First, they're often not well kept (Especially in older buildings), and could be weak, rusty, and may be unable to hold your weight (Hence my "trust" comment). Second, they're often found on taller buildings, and, if it's in bad shape, should the fire escape deteriorate beneath you, it will be a *long* way down. Third, most buildings with fire escapes are in cities, and most of those fire escapes lead to alleys or similar avenues, where there may be more zombies around than say, the rear, so one would be smart to ensure there *aren't* any waiting for them down below. Beyond those possible issues, if you have even the slightest confidence in your fire escape (Or more likely, you have no other option), then climbing down the fire escape is easily a better idea than running a possible gauntlet of zombies inside.

Rule #178: There's more than one way down.

Because fire escapes are fairly common and have their own specific problems, I chose to keep it separate. *This rule* details some quick and simple exits that you *may use* when in a pinch. If your apartment has a balcony or awning below the window, rather than having to deal with the zombies that could be inside, using either of these to mitigate the distance to the ground is likely a better option. If you're especially desperate, and *there are no awnings or balconies nearby*, you may have to do the simplest escape possible: Jumping out the window. It goes without saying (But for the idiots out there, I'm gonna say it *anyway*) that *these* options should only be used if a) There *AREN'T* zombies waiting for you at your landing zone and b) You can actually **MAKE THE JUMP**, *anything above two stories* is **HIGHLY UNADVISABLE, AS THERE IS EXTREMELY HIGH RISK OF GRIEVOUS INJURY OR DEATH** even *before any zombies get to you!!* If you're any higher than the second floor, just refer to Rule #177 and **take the damned fire escape!!** Don't be an idiot.

Rule #179: Window washer's trolley: The last refuge of a survivor.

I considered discussing this in Rule #114 ("Stay low"), but didn't really get a chance to. Luckily, it works *here*. As you may know, some skyscrapers have window-washers clean the windows using a motorized trolley to reach usually unreachable windows. If you couldn't follow Rule #114 for some reason and can't reach the first two floors the usual way, this may be your best bet to both reach the ground *AND* avoid zombies at the same time! Of course, this requires the building actually *have* said trolley and can be controlled *from the trolley* (Only being controlled from the roof doesn't do you jack).

> Side Note: It is possible that the trolley's cables only reach a certain distance down the façade of the building. In this case, I sincerely hope you have a good weapon at your disposal, as you'll need one to break through a window and attempt to reach the ground the old fashioned way (Obviously, a tough prospect or you wouldn't need the trolley in the first place, but it's possible, the circumstances may have changed on the ground floor). If it's *still* too perilous, you may have to go *back up* to the roof and go to plan B...

Rule #180: Plan B: A leap of faith.

I'm gonna start this off with the side note, for all the idiots out there, so bear with me.

> Side Note: ***ONLY** when you have **ABSOLUTELY NO OTHER MEANS** of safely reaching the ground without being swarmed by zombies and **ONLY** if the following is viable (I.E. **Doing this WILL NOT KILL OR CRIPPLE YOU!!**) should you **EVER** even consider doing the following. If you find yourself on an extremely high-rise building, **DO <u>NOT</u> DO THIS**... try to find a better way down.*

There, now that *that's* been dealt with, let's continue.

Only under the following conditions should what I'm suggesting be done:

1) If ***all*** other escape options are exhausted or reasonably deemed impossible to try without extreme risk of zombification.

2) You're positive you can attempt this ***without*** killing/ crippling yourself.

3) There is a building next to the one you're trapped in (Anything further than a few feet away from the edge of the building you're jumping from is probably too far and you'll likely miss and plummet to your death...unless, you're an Olympic long jumper).

4) Its ceiling is below the one you're jumping from (Not too far, you don't want to break your legs)

If you're lucky, the building you're jumping to may, in fact, be *connected* to yours and all you need to do is hop the wall or climb a short ladder, in this case, go for it, the building on the end may have *its own* fire escape you can climb down!

Now, when doing this always remember two things: There is a good chance that there are as many zombies in this building as there were in the one you left and you *SHOULD NOT* attempt this from extremely high-rise buildings as their neighbors are likely neither tall enough *OR CLOSE ENOUGH* for you to reach them. If you try this from such a skyscraper, you are doing so *ON YOUR OWN ACCORD!* Remember, I warned you ***NOT TO!!***

Chapter 4: Post Z-Day: Surviving and Thriving after the Apocalypse

Congratulations, you've survived the onslaught of Z-Day, and have managed to escape (Or avoid) your major population centers. But...now what? How are you going to live? What about everyone else? How are you going to take Earth back from the undead?

...Can you?

...Maybe. The following rules are intended to help you survive and eventually, <u>thrive</u> in a post Z-Day world. With a little luck, maybe you <u>can</u> rebuild civilization after all...

Rule #181: Find other people...<u>living</u> people.

Now, I know this is weird. I've spent the majority of this text trying to prepare you for survival *on your own*, but now we're talking *beyond* Z-Day -- if you want *anything close* to civilization, you *need* **people**.

Why? I've been okay so far? Won't more people be a liability?! Maybe. Honestly, joining others is risky: They can slow you down, conflicts can arise, or they could snap...*or worse*. But, more people can be beneficial: They may have stuff you need (Food, ammo, a *working* car), which go long ways to doing more than just scraping by. Also, they're extra sets of eyes/ears, or better yet, *an extra gun,* so you don't *have to* fend off zombies *yourself* all the time! Most importantly, they're somebody, to interact with; because eventually, isolation, especially now, can get to even the best of us. Even if you **hate** this other person, they're better than the ghouls waiting to rip your throat out. Basically, if you want to do *more* than just be a step ahead of the undead until you die, you must find some people; or else...you're in a long vacation in **Hell**.

Rule #182: Establish some kind of order.

Let's begin by saying the obvious (Or at least, what *should be* obvious), anarchy is idiocy; in the long run, it can only lead to xenophobia and likely a very brutal form of witch hunting mob rule, where the very suspicion of someone stealing supplies (Things which become extremely precious post Z-Day) leads to execution. To prevent this sort of breakdown in civility, the moment you become part of a group of survivors, you should try to establish some sort of simple order, even it's something so inconsequential as demanding that any borrowing/sharing of supplies be done with permission of the owner, so as to limit the potential of creating resentment or worse between members of your group. People who *get along* are a lot more likely to help each other than those who despise each other. Who knows? If they hate you, they may just *let you* get eaten…

Rule #183: Find/establish a semi-permanent base.

During Z-Day, I instructed you *NOT* to stay in one place, because (Especially in cities), eventually, it'll be surrounded by ghouls. As you try to survive *after* Z-Day, however, this can't exactly apply; eventually, you'll *need* a base, because eking out a living on the road **will NOT** be fun. While it's *possible*, over time, its deficiencies will catch up to you. If you have a base of operations, however, you can use what's around your base to sustain yourself. Taking a solid base, once you start trying to begin anew *after* Z-Day, is smarter than wandering around, unaware of what's next.

> Side Note: By "Base", I mean a solid structure with some means of keeping zombies as far from you as possible (If it securely segregates you and any zombies inside when you arrive, that helps, too), can withstand attacks from the living **and** the dead, has access to water, is reasonably far from population centers, and has multiple escape routes: Ideally, a high security prison, military base/government facility would be best. If your base lacks *at least* two of these, you may have to keep travelling until something good comes along…especially the water and keeping zombies away. **Those** are deal breakers.

Rule #184: Distance or Remoteness?

This one is tricky. When picking your base, you may have to choose between a place that's *far* from the nearest population center and a place that's *remote* relative to said population center, and, admittedly, deciding can be tough, as each factor has advantages and disadvantages. Luckily, I'm here to help sort out the pros and cons and maybe make it easier, let's start with **distance**: A place which is *only* distant usually has the advantage of a regular access road to make supply runs or escape a little easier (*Much easier* if there is a *back* access road the zombies haven't found). However, because there may only be open road between you and the population center you're trying to avoid, you risk having *nothing* to stop anyone, living or dead, from noticing you, meaning you may have to deal with zombies far sooner than you may have been prepared for.

Remoteness (Or at least how I'm using it) refers to something which is not simply *far away*, but rather, a place that's relatively far removed from civilization (A place located within a forest is a perfect example of how I'm using **remoteness** here). Being remote can give you the advantage of terrain: A forest can absorb sound far better than the open road, which means zombies either **arrive later** (Or later than if you had nothing but the road between you and the next town) or **not even know you're THERE!** Furthermore, it's far more difficult for a zombie to stumble through the woods than it is for one to march down the highway; anything that slows them down or disadvantages them is *good*. However, remoteness also has its downsides: If you need supplies from a nearby town (Which is a very real issue you'll face, especially early on), it will be a long and perhaps difficult trip, which can burn precious gas. Also, places which boast remoteness likely *don't* have a back exit, or if they do, it may be over difficult terrain which vehicles may not be able to cross.

Both of these possess benefits and detriments, but it's really up to you as to what sort of place you reside in after Z-Day. Now that I've ...made this more *complicated*...maybe this makes your choice...easier? ...Sorry.

214

Rule #185: Get rid of the squatters.

This is essential if you have any plans on sleeping almost anywhere with a roof overhead, and is *especially important* if you are planning in the long-term, as almost any shelter you choose to take will already have occupants of the undead persuasion, and **you** are responsible for seeing that these premises are only for people *living* in them. Now, how you go about this is largely up to what you feel is the best method for doing it. If your shelter is segregated and has several areas cordoned off from one another (Likely by its last living occupants as they fled) this *may* play to your advantage, as you may be faced with relatively small groups of zombies while other groups are kept safely behind locked doors until you're ready to deal with them. However you deal with them, make sure you **_do it_**, as you never know if a random zombie attack may force you to deeper into your base, and if you haven't cleared out all the zombies, you may find that the squatters have decided to take their displeasure at the accommodations out on *you*.

Rule #186: Good fences make good neighbors, great fences make dead neighbors!

First, do you have a solid base? If not, refer back to Rule #183 ("Find/establish a...base"). If you *do*, good, you're on the right track. Next, did you clear out any squatters? If not, get to it, or else those zombies will eat you out of house and home, literally. If you did, on the other hand, AWESOME! Now that you have a legit base that's safe *inside*, it's time to make it safe *outside*. What often gets lost in this situation is that, by fortifying the perimeter, it's possible to eradicate many of your potential attackers (Living *or* dead) without even firing a shot! Now, if you're still close to a population center, putting up your fence may attract visitors earlier than you hoped, so work as fast and as quietly as possible, that fence could mean the difference between life and death if things get *really* hairy.

Now I'm sure you're thinking *"What good is a makeshift fence gonna do me against countless zombies?!"* I'm getting to that. First, if you're going to do it, do it right: Get materials from a nearby hardware store like barbed or razor-wire, chain-link fencing and steel posts. There'll probably be zombies there, but most large hardware stores are in warehouses, which are roomy and can provide you lots of weapons to fight them with, so don't worry too much, just don't loiter. Once it's finished, take any spare large pieces of scrap metal you can find and adorn your fence with them. If the fence is sturdy enough, your spikes may impale and either kill or immobilize any zombies walking into it, making them easy pickings for a bullet or an axe. Again, a great fence may let you to avoid confronting the zombies almost entirely, so don't neglect it, it could save your life, or at least save you some bullets...which might save your life.

Side Note: If your base is a place which **already** *has* a real fence (A military base, a prison, etc.) most of your work is done for you, but it can always be improved on: Lining it with spikes is a good place to start, as we already discussed, but there is an even better method of improving it: *Electrification!* In the event these fences aren't *already* electrified (Which is entirely possible), some rudimentary wiring and a generator may turn your regular fence (Which by now should *already* be formidable) into an **electrified** fence, capable of overloading a zombie's brain with hundreds of volts of electricity! If it's enough to put down the living, chances are good it'll stop a zombie dead in its tracks.

Rule #187: Delegation of responsibility.

As you attempt to survive beyond Z-Day, it helps to make sure that everyone is busy (We'll cover why later) and since by now you should have some sort of base to be keeping an eye on, it helps to make sure you are evenly and properly delegating any work that needs doing. If, for example, you have someone who's had experience as a security or prison guard, they should be assigned to patrol and make sure there are no weak areas in your perimeter, if you have some who's a mechanic, have them make sure your vehicles are in the best condition they can be in the event you need to make a quick getaway, you get the idea. By assigning tasks to people according to what they're good at, you're putting such work in the best hands possible, and also, in the best hands to pass on such information to the rest of your group, which is important, as you never know if you may lose someone (Remember Rule #70, "Armies of One").

Rule #188: "All work and no play..."

That's part of a quote from the movie *"The Shining"*, and is relevant to this topic. Now, this may sound frivolous, maybe even dumb, but, to thrive after Z-Day, you *must* stay entertained. Imagine: You're in a strange place; reeking of death and clearly a scene of ***massive* carnage**. You're amongst **total strangers**. Outside, hundreds of walking corpses, each a more gruesome snapshot of Z-Day's brutality than the next, want to eat you *alive*, their moans greet you in the morning and serenade you to sleep at night. Worse still, everyday, you ***hope*** none have found their way inside...

Did you think about it? Good. Now imagine *living* this... every...*single*...**day.** *Living like this* for long can make you depressed or insane; neither is conducive to good health. In lieu of that, if you get a chance, take what you can find: Chess, a Rubik's cube, a Sudoku book (*Any* book, really), anything that'll keep all of you from falling into despair or insanity. Take a minute, have some fun; you're *still **alive,*** remember?

Rule #189: The Buddy System.

Remember way back in Rule #10, where we discussed bathroom etiquette? Well, in case you forgot; allow me to remind you the gist of it: Going to the bathroom puts you in an *extremely* **vulnerable** situation, and it would be best for you to go whilst accompanied by what amounts to an armed guard. Well, now that you are beyond Z-Day and are trying to live a life in its aftermath, this same concept should be applied to your day-to-day tasks, wherever they may take you. If, for example, you have holed up in a prison and are doing patrols to make sure you've cleaned out any "squatters" (See Rule #185), make sure you go with another (Armed) person, so that, should you run into anything unpleasant, you won't be dealing with it alone. In fact, everyone should be accompanied by a second armed person wherever and *whenever* they go.

It's not just for swimming anymore.

Rule #190: Trench Warfare.

One advantage we have over zombies is that, for the most part, they're dumb (But, you *should* try to see precisely just how smart they may be, a la Rule #28, "Know your enemy"). This means things we'd avoid; a zombie will likely stroll right into. Enter: Trench warfare. If you have the ability (More so if you **don't**) to build a sturdy fence (See Rule #186), you should dig a trench around at least the front of your base, funneling to a chokepoint (This makes fighting them easier by cutting their strength in numbers), at least six feet deep, lined with spikes made of any sturdy material you can get (Solid wood stakes or fence posts and large metal shards like those for your fence) preferably lined with something like tree sap to ensure whatever gets impaled there **stays there**. If you can do this, when the undead inevitably attack your base, this simple defense will likely remove a decent portion of their numbers…or at least leave them easy pickings for you, either way, if they're stuck in your trench, they're **not** knocking down your gates, and that's *always* an improvement.

Rule #191: Don't be "That Guy".

..."That Guy"? Who's "That Guy"?

Whether we know it or not, we all know who "That Guy" is: He is the person who will go above and beyond the call of duty to do whatever satisfies his own need for self-gratification even to the point of being detrimental *to himself.* For example: "That Guy" would steal a weapon from a fellow survivor as they're trying to keep the undead from entering their base, leaving that person defenseless. Similarly, "That Guy" would shirk his duty of ensuring no zombies enter a potential weak point he was designated to monitor, essentially giving the undead free pass into the base. And last, but certainly not least, "That Guy" would, when things are at their worst and the horde has broken through, steal a vehicle (Designed, or at least intended, to carry upwards of four people) and flee before anyone else had a chance to climb in, leaving them to either pile into whatever other vehicles, if any, are available, or...you get the idea.

Now, how does this affect him, you ask? Well, he could potentially have avoided a zombie break-in if he just **helped** the other person instead of abandoning them *and* stealing their weapon! Second, our third scenario may have never *even happened* had his lazy ass just taken the few extra minutes to make sure that weak spot hadn't become overrun by zombies. What else has he got to do? **WATCH TV?!** ...I don't think so... Lastly, "Thriving", as we have been attempting to do beyond this point, is nigh impossible, as he has left every other *living* person that he knows of to be mauled by zombies, eventually, with no one else around, he will likely starve to death, go insane and kill himself *or worse*, get outnumbered and eaten by zombies **HIMSELF.** Suffice to say, **do not, under *ANY CIRCUMSTANCES*,** be "That Guy". Remember, if you have any plans on "Thriving" and possibly getting rid of the undead, you need more than just yourself to do it, and any extremely selfish impulse you have, *BURY IT.* You have to remember that your actions not only affect the people around you, they'll eventually come back around and affect you, too, so don't do anything that'll jeopardize the survival of the group, or you *won't* live to regret it...

221

Rule #192: Always have an escape plan.

Now that you (Should) have a base of operations, you need to realize that as secure as it may be, one day, you may have to abandon your new home in a hurry, and as such, you need to plan out the optimal way you are going to do this. Even if it's something as straightforward as "Get outside, get into the cars, and drive!" it's better than running around like panicked animals (Much like people are likely to have done *on* Z-Day). Ideally, however, you will prepare careful escape routes for your base **well before** such a scenario ever comes close to happening, as well as contingency plans should certain exits be blocked. If you think ahead, certain disaster *may* just be avoided. If you have any further questions, go back to Chapter 2: Preparation, and look up Rules #80-83. I wrote those for a reason, don't ignore them...

Rule #193: Supply runs ain't no joke.

No matter what your situation is, whether you have a base or are trying to survive on the road, eventually, you'll need to gather supplies left over from a nearby community (Preferably a small, relatively open one, doing supply runs in major cities may be more dangerous than it's worth, but we'll discuss that later…). No matter what sort of place the nearest community is, there *will* be zombies, and it *will* be dangerous taking on such missions. Ergo, these should be planned very carefully, here are some suggestions:

1) Have an idea of what you're going for *before* you get there.

   Supplies are limited, no matter where you go, the dangers, however, *aren't*. You don't want to wander around aimlessly trying to decide where to look for the supplies you need. The sooner you get what you need, the better.

2) Take as much as you can reasonably carry.

   Since supply runs are dangerous, you should make them as infrequent as possible. You'll need something (A shopping carriage or, of course, a car) with good storage capacity to maximize your ability to carry supplies. Just remember, don't take so much as to slow you down.

3) Stealth and Speed: The keys to any good supply run.

   Whatever you need, wherever you're looking for it, you must be *quick **and** quiet*. This also applies to your weapons; it'd be smart to stick to manual weapons or silenced guns, if you have any.

4) Determine the best person/people to make supply runs.

What you soon realize about supply runs is that they require the fastest runners, drivers, the sneakiest thieves or the best zombie killers you have (Or ideally, some combination of all of these). In the event no one individual can do all of this, a team of two or three (Anything more might be a liability) may be the best way of achieving a successful supply run. Remember, ensure that the people you send to do this are *the best* you can get *to* do it. After all, you're gonna need them to do this ***again***.

5) Only enter cities if you have no other choice.

If you don't already know, see Chapter 3, Procedures: City Rules, for more. Remember, just because it's dangerous doesn't mean supplies are magically going to appear at the edge of the city closest to you to make it easier, you're still going to have to get in there eventually and get them!

6) If it gets too hairy, JUST RUN!

This…is…pretty self-explanatory. If the mission gets too dangerous, due to zombies or pursuit by other (Likely armed) people, just throw the supplies somewhere (If they're in the vicinity, a dumpster would be ideal, the zombies won't look there!). Then make sure to memorize the details of where you left it. As much as you may not want to, you *can* come back for it later.

Rule #194: Your new name is "Ol' McDonald".

If you remember Chapter 2: Preparation, I gave you a rule (#98, "The Need for Seeds" to be exact) about the value of seeds post Z-Day. Well…that's *now*. Do you *have* any seeds? If so, good; if not, during a supply run, find a gardening store to get things like tomato, bell pepper or cucumber seeds, or else, you may have an issue. Why? Eventually, your nearby community(s) *will*, for one reason or another, **run out of supplies**; it's inevitable. Then what're you gonna do… *cannibalism!?!* At that rate, you might as well be a zombie!! No. You're gonna *grow* your own food! Once you see progress in your veggies, plan meals around them. After you figure out simple vegetables, you can try to expand to things like apples or oranges (Depending on where you are), potatoes, carrots and grains, so you don't suffer from nutrient deficiency. By the way, you *may* (Read "**Will**") want to prepare for this eventuality *well before* the food you're scrounging locally runs out, that way you're ready when the time comes. You **don't** want to be waiting _a week_ for food, do you?

Rule #195: Rain, rain, DON'T GO AWAY!!

As mentioned in the previous rule, the supplies of the nearby communities *will*, eventually, run out, including water. Water, of course, is more valuable than bullets after Z-Day (Look to Rule #34, "Eat, drink…REPEAT!" for more info) and can be especially tough to find depending on your location (If the nearby lake or stream has become home to dead zombies, it is officially too contaminated to risk drinking from, unless you *want* to be a zombie), so you'll have to find other ways to get water, the best one being…rain. Again, depending on where you are, rain may be tough to come by (A desert area, for example, gets very little rain. Honestly, you may have to relocate to survive) but this doesn't mean you shouldn't prepare for it. No matter where you are, line the roof with tarps or buckets and collect as much rainwater as possible (If you're camped out on the ground, the principle is largely the same)! Whatever you do, remember to store it in a container quickly so it doesn't evaporate or stagnate, you may have to rely on this water for a while.

Rule #196: What doesn't know you're there can't hurt you.

I imagine you're confused, but think about it: Putting up fences, digging ditches, cooking food, all have the potential to draw a crowd. Now, I know, I know *"But YOU were the one who told me to **do those things!!**"* Hey, I never said things were going to be easy, **but**, with some simple precautions, you can mitigate just how conspicuous or loud you are, and doing so is important, as being either will draw *not only* zombies, but **living people** too, and they can be even more destructive than the zombies (If they haven't brought some in behind them)! Little things like building a wall around where you build fires, putting them out once your done (To minimize smoke), not working for too long at any one time (To prevent the zombies, or anyone else for that matter, from figuring out where the sound is coming from), hiding any vehicles you have from the main entrance of your base or camp (To avoid detection by passing raiders), and making sure that you have as little evidence of someone living there lying around as possible. While it's no guarantee *against* drawing attention to you, *not* taking these precautions will certainly go a long way *towards* doing just that.

> Side Note: I feel at this time, I should discuss disposal of *the bodies* of the undead, as you may have the idea to cremate them rather than just letting them rot in the sun. Now, while this *may* be a good way of disposing them, there *are* possible negative consequences to doing this, the worst being the possibility of actually *contracting* the disease by breathing in the smoke from their incineration, which, along with the massive flame, will be *INCREDIBLY CONSPICUOUS!!* While the zombies may not pay attention to it, it will draw potential raiders like the proverbial "Moths to the flame". You may be better suited creating a mass grave, but that also contains serious risks, not just of discovery, either. Whichever method you choose, try to be inconspicuous about it, the less the outside world knows about you, the better.

Rule #197: The ups and downs of winter.

We've already discussed how you can make the most of the relatively temperate times of year (Rules #194 & 195, to be more specific). Winter, however, is something completely different and presents its own set of challenges and advantages. If you're in an area which gets particularly cold and even snowy, for example, you may have to gather all your produce before the frost really begins to set in November. On the other hand, if your winter is more of a monsoon season, you may have to get to relatively high ground and prepare for war, as any destruction wrought on your base (If you're lucky enough to have one) may be an open invitation to any zombies left standing to invade. But don't fear, winter isn't all bad: With electricity being almost as precious as water (If you even have access to it), you likely have no method of refrigerating your food. Winter temperatures in northern temperate regions can often dip below freezing, which should be more than cold enough for any perishable food you may be relying upon to stay edible for an extended period of time. Furthermore, while we may have difficulty dealing with such freezing temperatures, being alive, we can still regulate our body temperature; zombies, however, CAN **NOT.** Think about this for a moment: If you have (per se) a week of temperatures near freezing, the zombies' muscles will likely stiffen to the point of immobility! With them potentially being frozen stiff, a team of strong people armed with sledgehammers, axes and guns could possibly **decimate** an entire army of undead in relatively short order! What's more, if a severe cold snap persists, you could potentially rid a decent portion of your surrounding area of the undead menace, inching you one step closer to eradicating the zombies! Just be careful not to trip on any zombies buried in the snow...

Rule #198: Your new name is "Ol' McDonald", part 2.

This is another difficult one, but no less important. As mentioned in Rule #28 ("Know your enemy"), you *do* **not** know what else the zombies eat or what else can carry the disease. Why bring this up here? Because, if you find yourself in the worst-case scenario, the zombies may have a taste for anything that breaths! This means that otherwise plentiful food sources like rabbits, deer, moose, etc. are now on the zombies' menu and could not only rob you of your backup food supply (Once you exhaust the supplies to be had in the surrounding area) but also swell their ranks with zombie animals!

If this is the case, you need to start raising your own livestock quick before they *all* become *zombified*! My suggestion would be to search the surrounding area for farmland during a supply run and attempt to collect things like sheep, rabbits, chickens and turkey (Which is best is dependent on what food supply you can most easily and safely provide them. Sheep eat grass, rabbits eat vegetables and the poultry usually eat things like corn and seeds) relatively soon after Z-Day, before they are all wiped out by the zombies! If you fail to do this, with nuts and another protein-bearing plants likely being difficult to come by (And perhaps even more difficult to grow) you may begin to lose muscle from a lack of protein, and considering how much activity a battle against the undead may require, protein is NOT something you can afford to lose. Suffice to say, if you want to outlast the zombies, you're going to need to learn to grow and raise *everything* you'll need to eat.

Rule #199: Women: Can't live without 'em.

Okay, gentleman, let me say this here and now: If you plan on trying to ensure that the human race *does NOT* die with you, you need the presence of at least one woman (Over 18, of course) to even **begin** to do this. Now, I don't want to have to explain the birds and the bees to you, but let's just put it this way: If *we*, as people, want to have more things like us, *we* can't just bite someone and *Poof* have another human being magically appear. No, we need...to...do...*other things*. And said "*Other things*" can't happen *without* women. So...yeah... you may want to keep an eye open for them...just saying. By the way, since you may want to make *multiple* people, you want to try and treat this whole circumstance like, I don't know, *a relationship?* Yeah, being a rapist isn't *exactly* how we want to perpetuate the human race, soooo...don't do it.

> Side Note: Ladies, this works both ways. I know there are <u>**some**</u> (Definitely not all, but some) of you out there who may think the world is better off without men, but, do you *really* want to live out the rest of your days knowing you're probably the *LAST PERSON ON EARTH?* I doubt it. So, as much as you *may not* like us, if *you* don't want humanity to end with you, you're gonna have to bite the bullet and learn to live with us guys, too. To the ladies who *DO* like us, thank you. I appreciate the fact you do NOT want our species to go extinct. You ladies are awesome.

Rule #200: Our most precious resource. Protect it at ALL COST.

As we close out "The Rules" for surviving Z-Day, think back, what is the ***most important*** thing that can help humanity survive? *Food?* Nah. Food's important, but it only prolongs the inevitable. *Water?* Nope. Water can only keep man alive for so long. *Shelter?* Good guess, it *can* keep *us* away from ***them***, but, even if no zombie crosses its threshold, it won't save *humanity*. *Bullets?* Oooh, close. Bullets *can* eradicate zombies quickly and efficiently, but, even if you kill *every* zombie, they aren't (And, frankly, never have been) the only thing that can kill you out there.

The correct answer is: Children. While all the other things mentioned are necessary for *you* to survive, if you're the last man alive, even eradicating the zombie menace from the face of The Earth means that you're *still* the last man alive: *Humanity* ends with you. However (And, on a side note, considering the theme of the last rule, you should've already known *this one*. C'mon, do I have to spell out *everything* for you?) if you, and any other groups of people you may now be surviving alongside, are able to raise kids to adulthood, you are guaranteeing that, long after the last zombie rots away, there *will be* ***living people*** still around to reclaim our world from the nightmare of Z-Day. As such, to ensure that that does indeed happen, you must protect any and all children (And pregnant women, for that matter) as best as humanly possible. I know there are some callous people who may note that while children are precious, should they die, adults can always make more. While this may be true, I would imagine that those people have ***never*** lost a child. The effects are devastating to their parents and, in the dire circumstances

of Z-Day, downright crushing to everyone in your group. Such a loss could condemn their parents to despair, and prevent them from trying again out of fear of losing whatever potential child they may have! So, it is **imperative** that, ***above all else***, you do everything possible to make sure all children survive to adulthood, so *they* can keep up the fight, and one day see humanity reclaim its home.

So, in short, yeah...it's kids. The answer was kids.

So, *those* are **The Rules**. Hopefully, the wisdom I have imparted upon you will be of help if that blackest of days, Z-Day, should ever fall upon us. I'll be the first to admit, I can't guarantee that you will survive past Z-Day, Hell; I can't promise **anyone** will survive past Z-Day. But, I think I've given you a leg up on everyone else who would otherwise be unwilling to accept that Z-Day is really happening and therefore, be unprepared for it. But I'm hoping this book has done more than that. I hope some of the simpler things I advised within this rulebook (Learning to back into parking spaces, becoming more physically fit, being observant, learning to navigate through nature and how to grow your own vegetables) have inspired you. Maybe now, every time you go to work, go into the city, take a train, go on vacation, you're thinking of what you would do should you find Z-Day has struck; how you'd escape from each of those places, and how you save yourself and the people you care about from becoming zombies. Maybe you're living a little smarter now that you've read *The Rules* than you might have been before. If I know that what I've written has made just one person think about how they'd get out of a zombie-infested city, then, I feel like I've done something good. Hopefully, I've succeeded.

About the Author

Liam O'Leary is a computer programmer by trade with a Bachelor's Degree from Bridgewater State University. This is his first book. He currently lives with his family outside of Boston.

Lightning Source UK Ltd.
Milton Keynes UK
UKHW041217110321
380174UK00001B/188